EXPOSED

AN ALEX DRAKE NOVEL

LEXXI JAMES

Exposed: An Alex Drake Novel
Version 2
Copyright © 2021 Lexxi James
www.LexxiJames.com
All rights reserved. Lexxi James, LLC.

Edited by the Utterly Extraordinary
Pam Berehulke
Bulletproof Editing

Independently Published.

Cover by Okay Creations

No part of this publication may be reproduced, distributed, or transmitted in any form or by any means, including photocopying, recording, or other electronic or mechanical methods, without the prior written permission of Lexxi James LLC. Under certain circumstances, a brief quote in reviews and for non-commercial use may be permitted as specified in copyright law. Permission may be granted through a written request to the publisher at LexxiJamesBooks@gmail.com.

This is a work of fiction. Names, characters, places, and incidents are the product of the author's imagination. Specific named locations, public names, and other specified elements are used for impact, but this novel's story and characters are 100 percent fictitious. Certain long-standing institutions, agencies, and public offices are mentioned, but the characters involved are wholly imaginary. Resemblance to individuals, living or dead, or to events which have occurred is purely coincidental. And if your life happens to bear a strong resemblance to my imaginings, then well done and cheers to you! You're a freaking rock star!

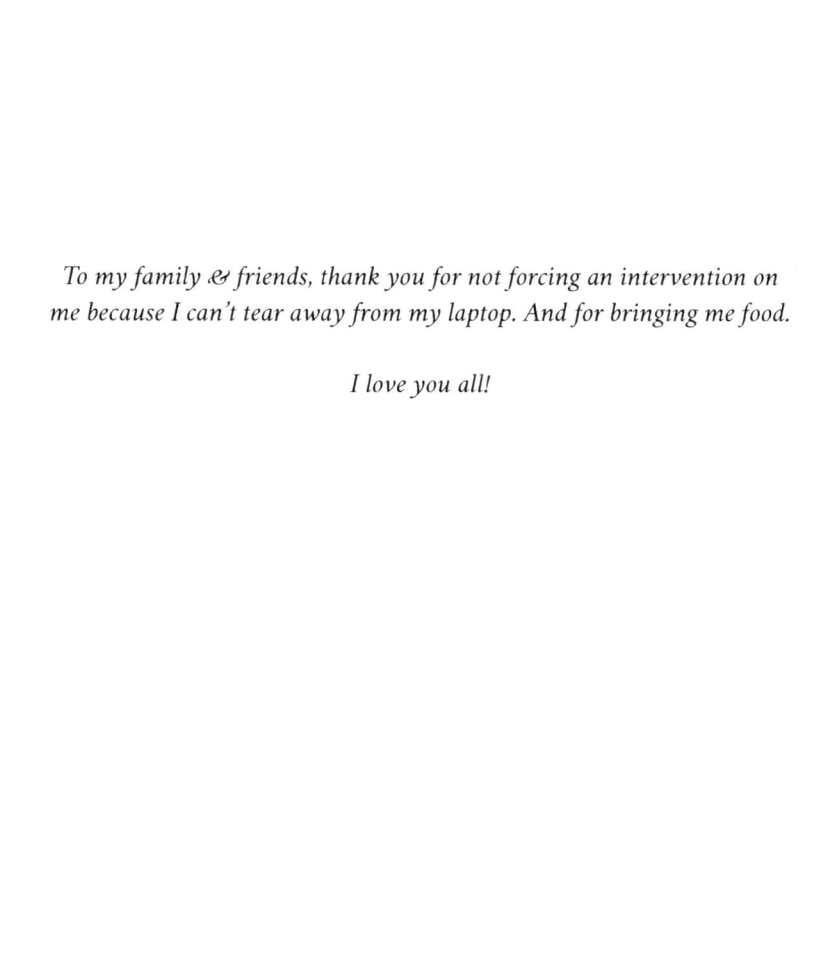

To my family & friends, thank you for not forcing an intervention on me because I can't tear away from my laptop. And for bringing me food.

I love you all!

CHAPTER 1

MADISON

"So, who is he?"

Madison caught the sly tone in her best friend's knowing voice. Sheila might be a reporter for the *New York Times*, but today her investigative skills were focused on getting the goods on Madison—her best friend and soon-to-be maid of honor.

Patiently, Sheila skated her finger along the rim of her half-consumed latte, her eyes dancing with anticipation as she waited.

Making a casual turn away, Madison focused on scanning the city streets from their perch at the corner café. Avoiding Sheila's see-right-through-you eye contact at all costs was pretty much impossible with the superhuman weight of her stare.

Madison shrugged, her lips breaking the leaf-decorated foam of her cappuccino as she savored an extra-long sip from the oversize mug. "I'm not sure what you mean."

"Right," Sheila drawled. As if ready to expose a cover-up, the diligent reporter leaned in. "Sure. The ridiculous smiling. The pep in your step. The glowing skin. I get it. You want to keep it on the down low. But you know that sooner or later, I'll figure out who he is."

Undoubtedly, Sheila was right. Always accurate in reading Madison's deepest thoughts, it didn't help that Sheila was a legitimate bloodhound when it came to sniffing out the truth. And keeping secrets was the last thing Madison wanted.

But sharing her secret with anyone, let alone an up-and-coming reporter like Sheila, was completely out of the question.

With a meditative breath, Madison let Sheila attempt her Jedi mind tricks, maintaining a stoic poker face. Madison rarely kept things from her best friend, and she knew Sheila was probably putting two and two together as they sat. With where Madison worked and how long she'd been floating on air, perhaps she was naive to think her new relationship with her boss would stay under wraps. But if Sheila figured it out on her own, it was fair game.

"Wait!" Sheila bounced in her chair, the riddle solved. "Holy shit, I get it. I know your big secret. You're dating . . ."

Madison sucked in a deep breath, ready for Alex Drake's name to fall from Sheila's lips. If Sheila connected the dots, Madison couldn't possibly deny it. Not convincingly, anyway. Instead, she braced for impact, her head already in an anticipatory nod of agreement before Sheila finished her sentence.

"A woman."

"Yes . . . *what?*" Madison's shy smile and modest blush vanished as she mentally repeated the last few lines of their conversation. *Did I just acknowledge being in a relationship with a woman?*

As Madison's head quickly shifted from nodding to shaking, Sheila's tone was reassuring.

"Look, if you're not ready to come out, I'm a vault. But really, we'd all be good with it." As Madison clasped her hands and placed her elbows on the table, leaning forward to correct the misunderstanding, Sheila piled her hands on top. "We're happiest when you're happy, and you're obviously happy."

Madison weighed the cards she held. On one hand, if she protested, Sheila and their other friends would just keep pestering her for her new significant other's identity. And it wasn't as if Alex had urged her to keep it under wraps. He hadn't.

If anything, he'd always made suggestions for them to go out. In public. Where absolutely anyone and everyone could see them. Together.

Just the thought made Madison's arms itch, but she resisted the urge to scratch. The truth was, she just wasn't ready to share this secret. Instead, she held it close, preserving the precious revelation like cherishing a wish in the seconds before blowing out the candles of a birthday cake.

On the other hand, perhaps playing along was the path of least resistance. Satiated for the moment, her friends would at least give her some breathing space. The ploy would buy a little time to get to know Alex better. In private.

And it wouldn't be an outright lie, would it? Madison didn't exactly say she was dating a woman. Sheila did. Madison could just, well, conveniently not deny it.

Tugging her hands delicately away like a Jenga piece, she gave her friend a smile.

"Well, um . . . I'm not saying I'm with a woman," she said, and Sheila blinked at her in confusion. "And I'm not saying I'm with a man . . . um . . . in particular." Madison's answer was becoming so tangled, she started confusing herself.

"So, you're not with anyone?" With a suspicious squint and lifted brow, Sheila took a slow sip of her drink.

Madison swallowed the lump in her throat, desperate to mask her every tell. Was it working?

As if sensing her uncertainty, Sheila stared back, studying Madison and searching her eyes for a clue to the truth.

I hate lying. Not just because it's deceptive and wrong, but because I suck at it.

Could she backpedal without tripping up? "Perhaps it's best I leave it at that."

"Leave it at what?" Sheila strummed her fingers on the table until she froze and her eyes lit up with enthusiasm. "Oh, you're *curious.*"

Sheila's slow, assured nod nearly convinced Madison to go ahead and confess. But she resisted. Wanting to avoid another ride on this merry-go-round of a guessing game, Madison decided to settle into her new label. At least for the time being.

I mean, it's true. By nature, I am a curious person. Sheila obviously inferred Madison's bi-curious status. *But that's not what I said.*

Newly attuned to the fine print, Madison spoke carefully. "I'm curious in general, sure." Her reply sounded much more like a question than a statement, but she went with it.

Squealing with delight, Sheila caught herself. Knocking her enthusiasm down half a peg, she leaned in closer. "Hey, I get it. I've dabbled in, you know, curiosity."

Choking on her froth, Madison widened her eyes, panicked that Sheila was undoubtedly ready to unburden herself with a rich assortment of endless and highly detailed visual descriptions.

Luckily, the waiter broke in. *Thank God.*

"Ladies, can I get you anything else?" Swooping between the two of them, he cleared the emptied plates.

Relieved, Madison breathed her sigh through a smile, never imagining how thankful she'd be for an interruption to girl talk. "Sheila, I've really got to get back to work." Reaching for her latest Hermès clutch, she pulled out the matching wallet, prepared to pay the bill.

"No, no, no, girl. This one's on me," Sheila said, handing the waiter cash. "No change, thanks."

"Thank *you*, ma'am," he said, delighted with the fat tip as he carried the neat stack of plates and cups away.

Both ladies stood. Madison stepped over, not fully prepared for Sheila's sweeping hug, which lingered as she happily rocked Madison to and fro before leaning back.

"And if you ever need to talk with someone who's, you know, been *there*," Sheila glanced at their crotches, "I'm here for you."

Madison followed Sheila's eye movements before snapping hers shut, desperate to kill whatever image might intrude into her thoughts. *That which has been thought can't be un-thought.*

"Okay, then," Madison said hesitantly. "I do so appreciate that, girl. Well, gotta run."

Madison checked her ten-carat diamond bracelet as if it were a watch, intent on scampering away. Extricating herself from the warm hug, she turned to head off, propelled faster with the light smack of Sheila's hand on her ass.

"You do you, girl!" Sheila called out a little too loudly for Madison's comfort. "And bring whoever you want to the wedding."

Madison waved back awkwardly, lowering her head while letting her thick tresses drape over her burning cheeks as she headed down the street.

As she approached the towering skyscraper that housed Drake Global Industries' New York City headquarters, she marveled at how her life had become an unbelievable whirlwind over the past few weeks. The dinners. The shopping. The traveling. It was overwhelming, but she'd done her best to take every bit of the opulence in stride.

Alex Drake had money. That much was clear. But as strange as it sounded, the lavish lifestyle this billionaire could afford her wasn't nearly as appealing as the man himself.

It was hard not to be a fangirl in his presence, but Madison cherished every here-and-there opportunity to get to know the reclusive man better. Those moments weren't showy or lavish, and they meant everything. How he managed to make mundane, everyday life feel new and magical was beyond her.

He adored her as no one had, as if she were the first woman to really be in his life. *And maybe I am.* But was there a reason for that? She tamped down her anxiety as much as she could, but it stubbornly remained in the back of her mind, threatening to come front and center at the slightest bump in the road of their relationship.

And as much as their blossoming relationship was wonderful, it was all so private. Extremely private. It wasn't as if they'd signed a nondisclosure agreement or anything, but neither of them pressed the other too hard to shout their relationship from the rooftops.

Madison wasn't eager to go public. She knew her credibility might fly out the window at DGI if water-cooler gossip hit the halls about her personal relationship with the boss. And Alex just seemed contented to keep her all to himself. Who could blame him?

And if things between them detoured from happily-ever-after, not only his image, but DGI's as well, might suffer an unintended consequence or two. Or a million. On top of which, their relationship was all so new. Only a few weeks.

Now, by the calendar of public opinion, some might argue this alone was more than impressive. It represented an Alex Drake Olympic-level world record. A notorious bachelor and womanizer, a Drake month of dating might as well be a dog year.

But worst of all, there was the secrecy. Maybe *secrecy* was too strong a term, but why was he waiting to tell her "everything else," as he put it?

What else is there? And what's with the book? And the photo? Or how we met? Or the whole making myself "at home" in his lap of luxury?

She'd noticed the novel *The Count of Monte Cristo* in his penthouse home, an inscribed gift many years ago from her grandpa Mike. Why would Alex have it? And the mysterious photo of her as a bright-eyed teen in one of the last moments with her dad before her parents' divorce. Why couldn't she remember it?

Shocking revelations had been piling up, kept just out of reach. When Madison demanded answers, Alex gave none. None in that moment, and none for the next month. But in thirty days, she'd have all her answers. All she had to do was stick around. And in a show of good faith, he handed her a contract. One she couldn't refuse.

I, Alex Drake, being of sound mind, do hereby agree that if I ever lie to Madison Taylor, everything I have and everything I own, including my personal and corporate holdings, will immediately and unequivocally be transferred to her for whatever purpose she deems fit.

Obviously, the man was insane. And just like that, Madison had moved in with him. How could she not? Because they were a perfect match—her crazy to his insanity. Could he possibly know he was the first man she'd ever lived with?

Normally, she'd have towering emotional walls built high around herself, preventing anyone from getting too close. Always protecting herself from a life where loss was inevitable. But with Alex, there were no walls. She'd eased into his life with cozy familiarity and had never been so comfortable. So at home. It should really bother her, but it didn't. At least, not enough for her to leave.

I'm falling. Hard. For a man I barely know. Which makes me certifiable. Possibly idiotic. But the thirty days I promised him are nearly up, so ready or not, answers are coming.

Despite all the other questions that pelted her mind daily, none of these was the most significant. The biggest remained the undisputed heavyweight question of all time.

Why me?

As quickly as these questions arose day in and day out, Madison just as persistently whack-a-moled them down. Per their agreement, all her answers were only a few days away. With that, she opted to focus instead on the monster of a question at hand.

Sheila's wedding was right around the corner. Madison was the maid of honor, and a plus-one would be required. The question of the hour danced through her mind.

Should I bring a man, or a woman?

CHAPTER 2

MADISON

Fidgeting, Madison stood as solemnly as possible in front of her boss's desk, desperate to keep a straight face.

"Let me get this straight." Alex sat at his desk, resting his elbows comfortably on the arms of his custom-made leather chair as his fingers steepled to his chin. A cocky-ass smirk spread across his face, drawing out a smile of her own that Madison couldn't hide. "You want to date a woman?"

"No!" she exclaimed, rolling her eyes at his misunderstanding.

"Oh, you just want to dip your *toe* in to test the waters. Or is this more of a *plunge* into the deep end?" Exaggerating a swan dive with one hand, he slid the fingers into the grip of the other, then suggestively pushed his fingers in and out of the clasped hole.

Madison shook her head, ignoring the heat his provocative miming stirred beneath her skirt. Sure, she was annoyed—more at herself than at Alex. Mostly because she couldn't hold back a laugh, no matter how she tried.

When Alex stood up, straightening and buttoning his blazer in that completely normal and sexier-than-hell way he always did, she bit her lip. He strolled around his desk to her, and her breath hitched as his warm and somewhat patriarchal hand landed her shoulder.

His expression somber, he cleared his throat. "Seriously, I support you. And if you need an innocent bystander to walk you through the delicate intricacies of pleasuring a woman, well . . . count me in." His selfless offer and cheesy grin were incorrigible.

God, he's such a man.

But he wasn't done. Lifting her hands, he held them against his chest. "Whatever you need, just name it." His deep tone coupled with those mesmerizing eyes somehow always made him less annoying and more adorable.

And don't even get me started on that boyish naughty grin.

Pulling her close, he lightly rubbed her nose with his. A delicate peck on her lips came next, which led to the most irresistible kisses down her neck.

"Well, there is *something* I need," Madison said, trying not to submit completely to Alex's intoxicating advances. *Though my panties are melted to oblivion.*

"Mm-hmm. Name it, you kinky little vixen." Alex made his way lower, rumbling out a delighted moan as he left a trail of searing kisses between her breasts. Cupping her fullness from the outside, he pressed her cleavage to his softly whiskered face.

Madison's breathing stuttered, partially from the touch of his lips rubbing across her décolletage, but mostly from the butterflies filling her stomach. "I need . . ."

"Yes? What do you need?" His tone was low and deep as he stood tall again, his hands making their way to the round curve of her ass, pulling her into him. His firm erection pressed against her skirt, coaxing her core and making her wetter by the second.

"I need a date for the wedding, but . . ." Exasperated, Madison let out a breath, averting her eyes. Her gaze dropped to his desk, seeing the penny she'd left weeks ago still in place. The heads-up coin stared back at her, reminding her to stay true to her feelings while guilting the hell out of her. She struggled to finish her sentence.

Alex pulled back, ducking his head down just enough to catch her gaze. Again, she tried looking away. His fingers lifted her chin, encouraging her eyes to meet his.

"But?"

A slow sigh escaped her lips, releasing a buildup of low, continuous pressure she'd been holding in.

"But I'm not sure we're ready for a public appearance." Searching his eyes, she forced out the last of her words. "Are you?"

With a fresh set of those damn nervous hives prickling up her arm, Madison waited, apprehension filling her as she waited for his reply.

CHAPTER 3

MADISON

Nervous anticipation hung in the air between them as Alex took his time giving her an answer. Too much time.

But, what if he actually wanted to go to the wedding with me? *Could I bring him? Would I bring him?*

The fame of Alex Drake's impressive corporate climb and financial status only slightly paled in comparison to his notorious womanizing. Those juicy topics would undoubtedly cause continuous gossip during the wedding reception, most likely overshadowing the wedding itself.

Topping it all was their relationship. A magical combination of attraction, seduction, romance, and even that elusive concept —trust. A show of trust handed to her on a silver platter by an irresistible man offering an insane contract.

It was a huge leap of faith—moving in with him, falling for him, a man she barely knew. What she did know about him was that Alex Drake was convincing. She could have anything and everything at her fingertips, and he asked nothing in return except to take a month to get to know him better.

Nothing to lose. Except maybe my heart.

Despite trying to get to know Alex better, she only saw the

things he let her see. Aspects of the man still eluded her, a side of himself or his past that he seemed reluctant to share. It kept him isolated. Shielded.

What's thirty days anyway?

Agreeing to wait a month for an explanation almost seemed trivial. But now she couldn't fight her curiosity. She needed to know what he meant when he referred to "the first time they met," some incident that despite her best efforts, she couldn't recall. She was also dying to know about the parts of him that stayed hidden. And everything else.

Those were his exact words. *Everything else.*

They echoed through Madison's mind, worming their way through her thoughts until nearly consuming her. Then that minute would pass and she could think of something else. Like Sheila's wedding.

With a deep breath, Alex swept a few wispy strands from Madison's face, studying her as she waited for his take on whether to take their relationship public. She looked up at him, unable to smooth the creases in her brow. If his walls were up, hers would be up too.

"I understand," he said so convincingly, she almost caved. "So, I get to keep you all to myself?" Scooping both her hands in his, he kissed each before pulling them to his chest. "I'm the luckiest man alive."

Ah, the dreaded diversionary tactic. I know it well.

Without much more leverage on whether they were taking their relationship public or not, Madison had two choices. She could either confront him outright about his thoughts on the matter, or she had to let it go. The awkward silence that followed made her reluctantly opt for the latter.

Giving her a peck, Alex offered a suggestion. "Hey, if you want to go down the path of bi-curiosity, I'll bet Gina knows someone who would love to be your *date*," he said, lifting his eyebrows and grinning devilishly. "Fancy night out, free food, maybe some heavy petting after a few drinks."

Playfully, Madison smacked his arm, pretending not to be annoyed at him. "Not exactly what I had in mind."

"Just offering suggestions. Can't a boy dream?" Alex gave her a mischievous look.

Madison gave him a pout that always had the opposite effect than intended. "Alex, I'm not taking a woman as my date, no matter how convenient it might be. I'm straight and I'm proud," she said, staunchly drawing a line in the sand.

Leaning in for a nuzzle of her neck, he murmured, "And don't I know it."

She made a feeble attempt to push him away before welcoming his advances. But before she could get swept away in the undertow of his passion, she stopped him, pressing her palm to his chest. "Wait, do you have time?"

He gave her a perplexed frown. "I thought that's why you dropped by during my one free spot today. Don't you have access to my calendar?"

"No," she said, nearly adding *crazy head* to the end of that sentence. Of course she didn't have access to his calendar. The man was a multibillionaire. A mogul. Obviously, his calendar was private.

Alex pulled away for an instant, tapping out a few effortless keystrokes at his computer before devoting his attention back to her. "You do now. Complete access." His lips were on hers before she could object. "And I've cleared my calendar."

The heat of his lips left a trail of seductive prints across her skin that cooled much too quickly for her liking, and the steady pooling between her legs promised a full surrender.

Softly, his lips brushed hers as his fingers made their way down her back to her skirt, then traced the tantalizing line separating her butt from her thigh, causing a shiver. That seductive finger worked slowly across her leg to the front. There, it lingered at her center, drawing lazy circles beneath her short, flowing skirt.

There was no keeping that man away from her newly moistened panties. He lightly stroked his patient fingers back and forth across her mound, until her wetness saturated the expensive silk undies she'd worried were too pretty to wear.

I can't confront him now. He's using his secret weapons to distract me. His touch. His warm breath on my skin. The Empire State Building hiding in his pants. This man knows my weaknesses. The biggest one being him.

Her head fell back but her gaze stayed on him. The heat of his hand was on her chest, and by the smile on his lips, the way her breathing raised and lowered her cleavage seemed to be to his satisfaction.

The steady ringing of his desk phone barely interrupted the pulsing of his fingers with its distinctive chime. Though the phone stopped briefly, it rang again. Simultaneously, his cell phone cut in with the ping of an incoming text.

"It might be important," Madison whispered.

"The hell it is." Alex softly growled, sliding his finger from the outside of her panties to beneath, taking his time enjoying the hot dew coating his fingertip.

Undeterred, he worked up and down her slickness, massaging her soaked folds before pushing a thick finger deep within her core. Her loud gasp couldn't be contained.

As her body rested against his other large hand across her back, he steadied her, letting her body relax and respond. His rigid finger pulled back and pushed in, over and over, as his thumb made its way to her clit, desperate for his touch. Her body rocked in his hold, chasing every touch against her needy, wanting core.

He pressed his tongue through her lips, both muffling her whimpers and enticing her to suck. The ringing started again, as did the text pings from the cell deep in his pants pocket. She had no complaints about the delicious vibration accompanying his solid cock against her sex, but the distracting tone was annoying.

Slowly, his fingers pulled out and his lips were off hers, but instead of letting her go, he pulled her in, scooping her up in an instant straddle around him. Effortlessly, he whisked her to his high-back leather executive chair, seating her gently in the worn comfort of it.

Finally, his cell phone rang. Alex snatched it from his pocket, his gaze fixed on Madison, his expression fervent and hungry but his tone businesslike and controlled. "I'm busy."

His calm words caused her to bite the smile from her lower lip.

He held the phone pressed to his ear, listening while he stroked Madison's thigh. One after the other, he lifted each of her legs over the armrests, and she let him as the silky fabric of her skirt fell away. His front-row view of her plump, ready pussy didn't make her shy. Eagerly, she watched his gaze darken. As his lips took a turn for the naughty, nothing mattered but pleasing him—right here, right now.

Her eyes widened as he knelt before her spread-open legs. Phone in hand, he silently lapped up her sweetness, not bothering to mute the line.

Madison let out a gasp as quietly as possible, hearing a muffled voice coming through the phone. Her master of multitasking emerged with her wetness glistening on his lips and chin.

Alex spoke into the phone with a deep, raspy voice, fixing his eyes on Madison's. "I'll come when I'm good and ready," he said before hanging up.

Finally.

Pocketing the phone, he returned to bury his face between her legs, his stubble rough against the tender skin of her inner thighs. In a long sweep, his tongue sliced into her, jolting her to cry out as quietly as she could. Desperate, she reached over her head, grabbing the headrest and using her strength to pull up just enough to spread her legs wider. Madison needed more, longing for him to fill her eager, aching core.

He took his time running his tongue back and forth before twisting it through her tightening walls. After a few lashes along her smooth crevice, he lifted his gaze, admiring her face as her heavy lids batted back.

"*Now* I'm good and ready," he growled, manipulating the chair to a recline.

He pulled a condom from his pocket, setting it on the desk next to that heads-up penny. She watched, hungering as he unfastened his belt, loosened his pants, and slipped them and his silk boxers to the floor. He wasn't exaggerating on that call. Every hard inch of him was ready.

Madison licked her lips, slid herself higher on the chair, and braced for his thick, heavy cock to press inside, stretch her walls, and make her his.

Alex leaned over her, first working two fingers through her wet tightness while circling her throbbing clit with his insanely talented thumb. She sucked in her lower lip and gently bit, breathing through the silent scream and panting as he unleashed his sweet torture.

"But they're waiting for you, and it's probably a huge deal," Madison said with a husky moan.

Alex lowered his head, groaning low in her ear. "Why, Ms. Taylor, are you referring to what I've got in store for you? Because I can't wait to present my huge deal to you."

With her breathing ragged and erratic, Madison struggled to speak. When his fingers slipped to just the right spot, her back arched and her body quaked under the attention of his controlled, intense movements.

"The, uh, business deal," she stammered out as reasonably and logically as possible, with what was sure to be a mind-blowing orgasm taking hold. "I—I know it's important."

But, oh my God, I'm close.

Close, but knowing Alex the way a girlfriend of about a month did, Madison was certain he wouldn't send her over like this. Not without him.

His hungry gaze was everywhere. The flush of her cheeks. The rise and fall of her chest. The lust in her eyes. But his rhythm didn't change. And it wouldn't. Not until he was ready.

"They're early. When they want ten million of my dollars, they can fucking wait. I've got a bigger priority," he said, slowly withdrawing his fingers to make way for his seeping rod.

He took barely a second to roll on the condom before burying himself inside her. She struggled for air as he pulled back out, then shoved every inch into her. She'd been desperate for that pleasure.

Laying his body over hers, Alex quickened his thrusts. His lips brushed hers, then across her neck until his breath was in her ear.

"I need you to come for me, Madison," he said in a low, gruff tone. A tone that carried her through each hard new thrust. "You can take all the sweet time you need."

His words set her on fire as an electrifying shiver raced across her body. She might have been able to hold out a short while longer, but his growled desire for her orgasm ignited something deep within her. Her body yielded to please him.

He pumped faster, timing his rhythm to the erotic circles his thumb made around her clit. Even when her pussy shuddered and her walls tightened around his thick cock, he kept going, bringing her to an even higher peak as he nibbled the sensitive skin on her neck.

Low, Alex demanded, "Now."

Her pussy shuddered, spasming tightly around his cock as her orgasm swept over her.

"Yes, Madison, yes."

She whimpered seductively, urging him on, and when he covered her mouth with his, she sucked on his tongue. Her wetness was still fresh, making her moan as she sucked. The fullness of his cock hit her everywhere as his body exploded in a series of husky sounds and forceful jolts.

He pulled back from her lips, both of them gasping. Catching his breath, he whispered, "You're the only woman I want, Madison. The only woman I will ever want."

Maybe it's the tender kisses he always gives me afterward. Or the way he says my name. Or maybe it's me, being shattered into a million blissful pieces and unable to fully pull myself together again. Whatever the reason, I believe him.

After a few minutes' rest, she looked into his eyes, gently stroking the dampness of his hair. "Should I slip out the back?"

Alex breathed out a light chuckle. "With me still inside you? I think that might draw a bit of attention." Resting his forehead on hers, he kissed her sweetly, then the sadist agonizingly pulled away.

Filling her lungs with a deep breath, Madison smiled as she undid herself from her spread-eagle yoga pose. Alex ducked into his office washroom as Madison sat up. Dizzy, she stayed seated for a moment, straightening her clothes as she scanned the floor. When Alex returned, he tapped her shoulder.

"Looking for these?" he said, teasing her while dangling a pair of panties from his sinfully talented finger. Before she could snatch them back, his hand closed around them as he whipped them away. "I need a distraction during the exhaustive meeting I'm about to start. These will at least make the day bearable. And I can use them to wipe my tears when I transfer ten million dollars to this startup," he said, dabbing his eyes with her panties before pulling them to his nose for a naughty inhale. A hum of pleasure vibrated from his chest as he savored her scent.

Before she could reach for them again, he pushed them in his breast pocket, an impromptu, crotch-up pocket square. Madison tucked them in a little deeper, smiling in flattered amusement. His strong hands cupped her face as he kissed her, melting her one last time.

As Madison made her way to Alex's private elevator, she was a little surprised when he waltzed in behind her. "Are you following me?" she asked coyly as she swiped her access card, selecting one floor down.

"To the ends of the earth."

This man will be the death of me.

He cupped her cheek, then caressed her neck as he held a kiss to her lips while the doors closed, then reopened a few seconds later.

"About the wedding," he said, holding her hand as she stepped off the car and turned. "Whatever you want, I'll make it happen. Just wish it."

The elevator doors shut on her handsome admirer, and Madison's smile vanished. Desperately, she wished for the one thing—the only thing—she wanted from him.

I wish I knew what you're keeping from me.

CHAPTER 4

MADISON

Having lost part of her morning to the man with the boyish charm and sinful hands, Madison bellied up to her computer, ready to roll up her sleeves and jump into work. But an email from Alex was all it took to distract her again.

As her heart thumped and butterflies fluttered, she opened it. The automatic text had her biting her lip.

ALEX DRAKE, CEO, INVITES YOU TO SHARE HIS CALENDAR

Madison couldn't possibly accept, but she couldn't *not* accept. He'd know, because important people like him always knew.

Despite her reluctance and apprehension, she tapped the return key, not realizing the system would launch today's schedule as soon as she did that. Ready to click the little *x* in the upper right corner to close the view, she found herself staring at one entry in particular.

SAMANTHA. EXECUTIVE SUITE 5010

Madison blinked at the screen, trying not to make too much

of it. But the meeting was private, marked with a little lock. Did he mean to give her full access?

It's fine. He meets with lots of people.

But all the other entries included the nature of the meeting. This one had nothing but a woman's name and a vacant executive suite that was only used for out-of-town VIPs who needed a desk.

Instantly, Madison called the only person who could give her perspective.

"Hey, girl," Madison heard along with a million clicks of typing through the phone.

"Hi, Sheila. I need to ask you a question. One of my colleagues is seeing someone—"

The typing stopped. "Oh, this is gonna be good. Cheating, right?"

"What makes you say that?"

"Because it's my freaking specialty."

Ignoring the comment, Madison pressed on. "Anyway, she found a suspicious meeting with another woman on his calendar."

"Uh-huh," Sheila said, taking that all-too-familiar tone of *I know where this is going.* "How did your colleague *accidentally* access his calendar?"

Confident, Madison said, "It wasn't an accident. He gave her access. Which he obviously wouldn't do if he was hitting it with someone else, right?"

"And this is why I always say men do this to themselves. Dumbass."

It took all Madison's willpower not to defend her man in that moment.

"Let's give the man the benefit of the doubt," Sheila said. *Yes. Perfect. Exactly what we should do.* "How long have they been dating?"

Sheepishly, Madison muttered, "Not long," as her head fell to her hand.

"Well, how long have they known each other?"

"Um . . ." This wasn't looking good. "They kind of . . . sort of . . ."

"Just met. Got it. What's the name of the other woman?"

"Just to be clear, we don't know that she is *the other* woman." Madison reread the entry. "The appointment is with Samantha. Why?"

"No reason. But *Samantha* sounds sexy. And where's the meeting?"

"In an office."

"Mm-hmm."

"Don't salivate. This isn't a story. Just a colleague looking for advice."

"I only salivate when I know I'm on the right track. It's sort of why I love my job."

Madison sucked in a breath, regretting the question before it left her lips. "What would you do . . . if it were you?"

"Maddi, let me get this straight. You're asking an investigative reporter what she would do when confronted with a situation ripe with the overwhelming stank of suspicion?" Letting the silence sink in, Sheila huffed. "Need I say more?"

"No," Madison said, deflated.

"Besides, she could drop by. If she works in the building, there's no harm in stretching her legs, right?"

"I guess not." Madison could easily rationalize the harmless break to get away from her screen.

"Any chance of a front-row seat? I could even grab my camera, snap some shots. Maybe this guy will think twice when his face is plastered all over social media as a cheater cheater, pumpkin eater."

Still protective for reasons she couldn't explain, Madison said, "Sorry, girl. She sort of wants to tackle it alone."

"Just let her know. Keying a car is an actual crime. And my way is so much more satisfying."

"Sage advice." *And a hard pass. On both accounts.*

"Anytime. Oh, my editor's coming. Gotta run. Later."

"'Bye." Madison sank back into her chair to think about it. She clicked the *x* in the upper right corner, closing Alex's calendar, but still saw the words in her mind's eye as clear as day.

The discouraging fact was that she barely knew Alex. She had to be smart. Do this, or always wonder about it.

I'll just walk by.

Saying a silent prayer that she was blowing this whole meeting with Sexy Samantha out of proportion, she waited until the indicated time and began her own investigation. Sticking with a leisurely, casual stride, she headed down the halls of DGI, straight for a room with the door closed and the glass walls frosted. Or mostly frosted.

After a minute of surveillance, she discovered a discreet place to peer through a small strip of the glass wall that was transparent. The problem? It was big enough that anyone inside the room looking that way would see her. And yet it wasn't enough of a deterrent to stop her.

Wide-eyed, Madison wasn't sure what to make of it. There was Alex. And apparently, there was Samantha.

Madison had to admit that Samantha *was* sexy. Seated with her luxurious locks spilling from a ponytail, the woman had both her hands in Alex's, and all Madison could do was watch.

CHAPTER 5

MADISON

With wide eyes and her palms pressed to the cool glass, Madison studied the two, having no idea what to make of it.

Alex sat at the small round conference table. Not wearing his blazer and with his sleeves rolled up, he seemed to be in a serious conversation. One that apparently involved tremendous amounts of support from Sexy Samantha. And hand holding.

After another minute of watching their discussion and having zero luck with reading lips, Madison's eyes widened as Alex jumped up from his seat. Charged with excitement, he raked both hands through his hair as he spoke with a booming voice.

Unconcerned but attentive, Samantha didn't react or seem overly concerned with his outburst or his sudden sporadic pacing. Having spent whatever emotions he had on the moment, he returned to his seat and back to Samantha.

With a keen eye, Madison studied the two.

Were they working? Were they friends? Perhaps they were friends. Which would explain how Samantha maintained a charmed smile during his outburst. And how her words could soothe him, convincing him to relax back in his seat. The whole hand-rubbing thing she was doing could be considered sweet.

Or seductive.

Or maybe I've got to stop asking Sheila for advice.

Determined, Madison shook her head, pressing her ear hard against the glass. She was barely able to make out two words.

"Not enough."

What wasn't enough?

Was it about work? Or them? Is there a "them"?

Alex and Samantha's ongoing conversation was fairly uneventful. Even boring. No *gotcha* or *aha* moments. For that matter, it looked like a friendly conversation that could have happened any number of places in the building, such as the lobby. A conference room. Alex's office.

Why here?

Madison looked up and down the halls. Only then did it occur to her that no one else had passed by. This wing was quiet. In fact, it seemed mostly vacant, safe from prying eyes.

Well, except Madison's.

This is ridiculous.

Before she could step away and return to her real work of the day, Alex stood. He rolled down his sleeves and checked his watch, the meeting suddenly over. That's when Samantha stood too, then wrapped her arms around him for a hug.

Despite the flush overtaking her cheeks, the erratic pounding in her chest, or her feet being half a step from bolting, Madison took half a breath. Then a full one. This hug was happening, but nothing else. No hand on the butt. No boob grab. Not the remotest sign of a kiss.

Sexy Samantha had gone out of her way to give what could be perfectly described as a bro-hug. Barely leaning in. Ass out. Pat to the upper back. No contact whatsoever with anything south of the equator. Samantha kept the hug brisk and deliberate, backing away with a polite smile and a fair amount of distance. A far cry from first base.

Madison was ready with a *friend zone* ruling until they opened the door. His voice low, Alex said, "I'd walk you out, but you know how it is."

"Oh yes," Samantha said with an elegant laugh, her voice soft and raspy. "Being seen with me? I know a few dozen reporters who'd love that scoop." She winked, as vixens often do, and hurried away.

After he spent a few moments straightening his tie and slipping on his blazer, Alex left the room. Madison counted thirty seconds before heading the same way herself, confident she'd avoid anyone at all as she took slow steps to the elevator, her head down as she contemplated everything she'd seen.

"Madison?"

Caught, she froze and looked up, but managed to speak. "Alex. Hi."

His hands in his pockets, he took a quick glance around and stepped closer, so much so that she was forced to crane her neck to take in the intensity of his dark eyes. Heat poured from him, blanketing her body.

"What are you doing here?" he asked.

Spying. "Stretching my legs."

He bent quickly, his lips meeting hers in a quick peck before she could object or speak, or move, or breathe. "It's perfect I'm seeing you."

"It is?" she whispered, uncertain.

"I have a surprise for you. There's an overnight bag in your office with a fresh change of clothes. We'll take off whenever you want today for a long weekend, and will come back Tuesday night."

"But I've got a few meetings . . ."

"I've got a few meetings myself . . ." Alex's lips nibbled hers, silencing her, his hands still in the pockets of his slacks. Tenderly, his mouth moved over hers, brushing her full bottom lip before teasing her with barely a lick. Just a taste, a delectable hint of everything her body wanted more of.

Madison could feel the growing wetness between her legs. Then he backed away, creating distance between them with the opening of the elevator doors.

A man with a wheeled utility cart exited, nodding politely as he passed the two.

"After you." Politely, Alex extended an arm, then patted his jacket with a huff. "Dammit, my phone. Madison—"

"Go," she said, realizing he must have forgotten it in the room.

Disagreeing with a firm shake of his head, he tried stepping into the elevator with her, but she pressed her palm to his chest.

"You've spent way too much time seducing me today."

Alex kept an arm on the elevator door, preventing it from closing, but setting off a faint chime. "Oh, I've just begun. As soon as you're done today, head to my elevator, hit *R*, and the seduction will continue."

With that, he released the doors, waiting until they fully closed before stepping away.

CHAPTER 6

MADISON

Well past five o'clock, Madison worried less about Samantha and more about how long Alex must have been waiting. Her last meeting of the day ran late, and couldn't exactly be interrupted with *Gotta go—secret rendezvous with the CEO. Later, gators.*

And the bag Alex had packed for her and left in her office was missing one particular item. Madison wasn't exactly used to frolicking around commando, but she was already in a rush. For this man, she suspected she'd probably do a whole lot more.

She bounced impatiently on the balls of her feet as the elevator lifted in agonizing slow motion. After about ten years, the doors opened to a rush of crisp, fresh air on the rooftop, high above the streets of Manhattan.

Ahead of her, Alex leaned back against the glossy surface of a luxurious fifty-two-foot black helicopter, unhurriedly scrolling through his phone.

He looked up. "Ready, beautiful?"

Elated, she ran full force into him. His arms wrapped tightly around her, willing her into a long, soothing kiss.

"For absolutely anything," she said, pressing another eager kiss to his lips.

She savored it, sinking into this and every kiss as if they both felt the same—like each might be their last. Under the late-day sun, they took their time, letting the kiss linger before slowly melting away.

"Well," he said with a recovering breath, "if that's the kind of greeting I get with this, I'd better let you sit up front with the pilot."

Madison couldn't help planting her eager lips back on his, filling this kiss with all the energy and excitement of the new adventure to come.

Gently, Alex pulled back from her smiling lips, letting his finger brush her full lower one, plump and sensitive at his touch. "Hey, if we don't stop now, we'll never leave." He lifted her chin for another soft peck, then moved to unlatch the door and help her in.

Madison settled into the leather bucket seat, taking in all the unusual gadgets and brightly lit buttons. She admired how they crammed the console, knowing each had a mysterious purpose that must take years to master.

In a few long strides, Alex was on the other side of the aircraft, entering to take the seat next to her. "I'll just sit here for a minute while you buckle in."

Madison took the cue while he handed her a headset. With a short examination of it, she slipped it on. Casually, he pulled on an identical one.

"Can you hear okay?" he asked into the attached mic.

"Yes, perfectly."

Her eyes growing in wonderment at the sight of so many switches and doodads, she eagerly awaited the pilot who could explain it all.

Why might some light up while others didn't? What were the dials for? And what was with the joystick? Staring, she considered how the long arm that extended from the floor was both massive and suggestive, but she managed to tame her naughty smile.

The displays and controls captured her interest until her gaze drifted to Alex. Puzzled, he let out a small huff of impatience as he considered the console.

"I wonder what this does." Carelessly, he flipped a switch, and the display turned on. "Hmm, what about this?"

Another flip, and a few more buttons lit up. Madison caught the grin that instantly gave him away.

Clicking his own seat belt firmly in place, he asked, "Are you *sure* you're up for anything?" Alex seemed to enjoy surprising her, sharing secrets little by little to reveal more of himself.

Captivated, she asked, "You're the pilot?"

He flipped a few more switches and checked some levers overhead, then his delighted eyes met hers while he spoke into his headset. "November-One-Seven-Delta-Golf departing the Manhattan downtown district. Request permission to transition your airspace to the north."

Another voice broke through. "November-One-Seven-Delta-Golf, stand by."

Alex took her hand and brushed his lips softly against her knuckles, sending a tingle up her arm.

"November-One-Seven-Delta-Golf, you're cleared into the class bravo airspace. Cleared to transition to the north. Maintain twenty-five hundred feet. Safe flight, Mr. Drake."

Still holding her knuckles to his lips, he kissed them and replied, "Thanks, Neal. Give Carolyn and the kids my best." He set Madison's hand back on her lap, and they were off.

Holding her breath, Madison watched as the DGI symbol on Alex's midtown helipad shrank into the sea of high-rise buildings. As they rose high above Manhattan, everything about the biggest city she'd ever been in looked strangely small.

"If there's anything you want a second look at, just let me know."

She nodded, too enthralled to speak. Though she'd flown on planes a few times, this vantage point was entirely different. So much more was visible—like being on the wings of an eagle midflight over the city.

His voice rumbled low over the headset. "Take the cyclic."

Madison whipped her head around, seeing him motion to the joystick.

"Go ahead. Just hold it steady." When she slipped her hands nervously around it, Alex clasped both hands behind his head. "I'm just gonna take a little nap."

"What?" she cried, her pitched voice filled with terrified elation.

"You're doing great. You've got about twenty minutes, then I'll take it back as we get closer."

Her grin widened, and Alex gently swept her hair back behind her ear. She beamed even more, realizing he was getting a better look at her. She loved the way he looked at her, but it was these penetrating gazes that somehow always turned up the heat in her cheeks, painting them in a warm blush.

After a while, the buildings became fewer and farther between, overtaken by the lush green of grass and trees, broken here and there by the blues and whites of rivers. Alex's stroke on Madison's hand nudged her enough to relinquish control.

Based on the direction of the setting sun, Madison knew they hadn't veered from their original northbound heading. Though she'd never been here, the stunning beauty of the land was instantly recognizable. The Adirondacks welcomed her, instantly giving her a sense of peace and relaxation.

She pulled in a breath as she took it all in from her bird's-eye view. "It's gorgeous. Are we going camping?"

"We are. We'll be camping in a six-bedroom luxury cabin on a lake owned by a friend of mine. But if you prefer something more rugged, I'll do my best at moose calls."

Madison pretended to sigh with disappointment. "I guess a

luxury cabin might do. But only if there are s'mores," she said, unveiling a giddy excitement that always seemed to encourage him.

Alex reached back, retrieving a small paper bag from the seat behind them. He handed it to Madison, who opened it to stare in disbelief. Inside were chocolate bars, graham crackers, and some of the biggest marshmallows she'd ever seen.

"Oh, you got me s'mores?"

Aghast, Alex stared at her. "No, I got *me* s'mores." He slowly pried the bag from Madison's hands and returned it to the back seat. "But I could be enticed to trade."

"Trade?"

He straightened and did his best at being aristocratic. "Well, I happen to be a collector. A collector of rare undergarments."

"Rare?" she asked, genuinely perplexed. *Like, vintage?*

"Rare, indeed. You see, I only collect undergarments that have touched the erogenous zones of your body."

"Oh, I guess I do see."

Madison's expression dropped, her downturned mood enough to prompt him to grab the bag and eagerly return it to her hand. Still in character, she declined, realizing Alex hadn't intentionally forgotten to pack her panties. It was an oversight. One she intended to use.

Through the playful veil of her thick, batting eyelashes, she gave him a remorseful glance with an exaggerated sigh.

"Well, I was really looking forward to some of that chocolatey chewiness. But at the moment, a trade's just not possible." Licking her lips and adding a full pout, she pulled in a deep breath. "Sadly, I'm not wearing any, um, collectibles."

His creased brow and tight lips transformed to a wide-eyed grin. And amongst the incoming evergreens and fresh air, Alex suddenly had two cyclics to contend with.

CHAPTER 7

MADISON

Through a break in the forest, a plush green glade came into view. Two people—a man and a woman—waved. The woman's wave eclipsed the man's, excited bursts with both arms as she jumped several times to get their attention. With a shy smile, Madison waved back.

Behind the friendly duo was a stunning property. The magnificent structure and likely architectural feat was what Madison assumed Alex meant by the "cabin."

The front of the lodge-style mansion featured abundant tall windows separated by log walls and large stone accents, while the back of the fortress overlooked the still blue of a crystalline lake. Circling for only a moment, the helicopter hovered in for a landing.

Waiting out the unforgiving gusts kicked up by the rotor blades, the couple hurried from their distant spots to greet them. The man and woman, dressed down in flannel and jeans, both contrasted with the elegant home and complemented it. Their smiles beamed as they greeted Madison and Alex.

Alex hopped out first, kidlike in leaping off the platform. He jogged around to Madison's door and lifted her by the waist, spinning her onto the ground.

With a swarm of butterflies flitting in her belly, she smoothed her hair and tugged at her outfit, eager to make a good impression. Aside from Paco, her new friend and Alex's right-hand man, these were the first of Alex's friends that he'd introduced her to.

As the couple approached, the burly man wearing glasses, a scruffy beard, and a warm smile blurted, "So, this is your sexy new baby!"

Madison felt every bit of the heat rising in her cheeks, certain everyone could see the redness warming her face. Instantly, the auburn-haired woman tugged her into a warm embrace.

"He means the chopper," the woman whispered in her ear, and relief poured from Madison in an audible exhale. The men were too engrossed to notice, making their way to the helicopter.

Madison overheard Alex explain it was the Sikorsky 76-D, and that custodial rights could always be arranged for a favor.

Just how many people owe this man a favor?

"Hi, I'm Jessica Bishop, but everyone calls me Jess. And you must be Madison." Jess gestured for them to head to the house, looping a sisterly arm through Madison's as if they were long-lost relatives catching up. "We've heard so much about you."

You have? Madison concealed her surprise and focused on the incredible home they were strolling toward. "Wow, your place is magnificent."

"I know, it's a bit much, but the land has been in my family for years. I come from a long line of mountain people. Simple-life lovers. Then Mark swept me off my feet, and after years of persistence, convinced me that a *log cabin* would suit the space well. Four years and three architects later, here's Mark's tribute to the simple life. Our home away from home for years now."

Jess presented the palace as only a knockout of a spokesmodel would. Her beauty was natural and effortless, unpretentious yet stunning.

Seeing Jess in this light, Madison guessed she was in her forties, a gorgeous beauty loosely concealed beneath her casual clothes. Without a bit of makeup, she somehow reminded Madison of what Marilyn Monroe or Ann-Margret might have been like on a lazy weekend between sex-bomb shoots.

As the men headed back, raucous with the laughter of an obvious tight bond, Madison turned to greet them. Extending her hand in a do-over, she relished a restart to their conversation, unconcerned of any possibility that the handsome lumberjack might lead with a comment on her degree of sexiness.

"Jess was just telling me about all the work you put into this beautiful property. It's amazing, Mr. Bishop."

The mister might seem formal, but after years of working in the service industry, old habits died hard—always address people formally first, until asked to do otherwise. Sometimes it felt stiff and uncaring, but she always warmed it up with a genuine grin.

As he gripped her hand firmly, his reaction became pained. With sudden exaggerated force, both of Mark's hands flew dramatically over his heart, as if struck by a crossbow at a hundred yards.

"Et tu, Brute? Et tu?"

Madison blinked rapidly, concerned about her apparent faux pas and wondering what the hell she'd done wrong, but Jess and Alex just laughed.

Unsympathetic, Jess laid a few firm claps on her husband's back, chiming in with a big, cheesy grin. "Don't mind him. It's hard for the male ego when we marry them but won't take their name."

Alex slipped his arms around Madison's waist, pulling her back against the heat of the front of him. Instantly, she relaxed into his embrace, receiving a few quick kisses to her temple. "You can just call him Mark. Though I hardly recognized you, man. You look like a grizzly bear with glasses."

"Hey, the mountain life changes you, brother." Mark gave that shaggy beard of his a few strokes, making Madison wonder what Alex would look like if he let his scruff really go. "No shave in almost two weeks. The longest I've ever gone. But I'll clean up in a few days before heading back to the office."

With a knowing glance at Madison still wrapped in Alex's arms, Mark continued. "Well, Madison, welcome. It's great to finally meet you, and to see Alex so happy." He shifted to give Alex an accusatory squint. "And I'm sure you're glad to be up here without feeling like a third wheel."

Alex grinned, shaking his head. "Hey, I was *very* happy to be a third wheel. Dragging me up here wasn't exactly roughing it. And I wasn't bringing someone here until it was the right someone."

The wild thumping in Madison's chest left her speechless.

They're all friends. Good friends. And the place has been here for years. What does it mean? Something? Anything?

Trapped between confusion and elation, she turned in Alex's arms, searching his eyes for an answer. Without saying a word, he pressed his warm lips tenderly to hers.

Perhaps he said more than he intended. Is he ready for this? Am I? Am I making too much of it?

Maybe this was more, more than either of them were ready for, if they really sat down and mapped out all the plusses and minuses of diving headfirst into the chemistry that sparked like the Fourth of July between them.

But everything was perfect. Comfortable. Right.

In the surrender of their growing kiss, the world melted away. Madison barely noticed as Jess and Mark turned and walked toward the house, giving her and Alex as much time and space and sweeping kisses as they needed.

CHAPTER 8

MADISON

Dinner prep that evening was nothing like Madison might have imagined. Alex and Mark spent an hour slaving away in the kitchen while Jess and Madison got to know each other better.

Despite her repeated attempts to chop vegetables or clean up, the men continued shooing Madison away, insisting she relax and be pampered. On her last attempt, Alex promptly marched her butt out of the kitchen, sending her off with a kiss, a generous pour of aged cabernet, and the sweetest swat on her backside.

Amused and apparently accustomed to being waited on hand and foot by the two otherwise high-testosterone alphas, Jess encouraged her to give in. Reluctantly, Madison succumbed to the deep berry swirl of the red in her hand, headed to Jess for a clink, and finally curled up alongside her on the overstuffed sofa.

"Madison, can I ask you, do you come from a service background? Food services or hospitality?"

Madison gave Jess a bashful shrug. *Is it that apparent?* "Yes. That's pretty much my entire background. How'd you know?"

"Me too. It's written all over your need to help in the kitchen. Trust me, while you're here, the boys won't let you lift a finger."

"Wow, we'll have to drop by more often."

"Anytime. I love the girl time, and I rarely get it up here."

Jess was easy to talk to, unpretentious and open, and she shared freely about her life. She wasn't the kept woman some might think, and the nonprofit she'd started years ago helped vets to that day. It also happened to be how Jess and Mark met.

"It was a fundraiser. Love at first sight, which might have been clear to anyone watching, but denial was my game," Jess said, her giggle equal parts sentimental and naughty as she reminisced. "We were strangely inseparable. I called myself his 'heart hostage' and kept trying to push him off. If I vanished off the face of the earth, a stampede of lady contenders would've been vying to be by his side. But Mark was just so damn tenacious."

Madison sighed with pleasure. *Is there anything better than a love story?*

"Nobody thought it would last," Jess said. "I'm pretty laid back, and couldn't care less about how many bazillions he had. And when we married—the mountain woman and the megabucks tycoon—it was hard to keep up with all the hushed chatter. How long would we last? How much would I get if we divorced? Five different divorce attorneys handed me their business cards when I was out shopping. They followed me and found me, like stalking was cool so long as it was in my best interest."

"That's insane."

"Mark wanted me to have a bodyguard, but there was no need. I grew up with five brothers who taught this girl how to aim for the groin and make it hurt."

Taking a long sip of her wine, Madison reminisced for a moment about her own brother and the lesson Jack gave her on how to successfully deliver a knee to the jewels. It made her smile.

"But at the end of the day," Jess said, "it's Mark's passion that drives him, not his profit. He knows that I'm in love with him, not his billfold. If he lost everything tomorrow, he'd still have me. And somehow, I feel like it's the same with you and Alex."

"Oh." Madison buried her elation at Jess's words behind a restrained smile and another sip of wine. Could she and Alex really be on par with Jess and Mark? "Why do you say that?"

"Well, for starters, you work."

Madison shrugged. "At Alex's company."

Finishing off the glass, she set it down and grabbed the nearest throw pillow, hugging it to her chest. Curling her feet up under her, she let the effects of the bold red set in as she relaxed back into the plushness of the sofa.

Jess gave her a knowing look. "Yes, but if I know Alex, and I'd like to think I'm one of the few who know him pretty well, I'm sure he's made it abundantly clear that you don't have to. Am I right?"

Madison nodded, trying to hide her surprise. Nobody knew that Alex had offered her the lap of luxury. *His* lap of luxury. And as alluring as his offer was, she'd declined it over and over again, afraid of letting herself fall for a man with the reputation of keeping his women temporary and at arm's length.

Selfishly, she had to have more than the fleeting spoils and disposable consequences of being a kept woman. Keeping her job was a small step to having all of Alex Drake, while holding on for dear life to herself.

"And yet you continue to work. My guess is you do it to learn and grow as your own person, driven by your passion. Same as all of us." Crossing one leg over the other, Jess took a sip of her wine and leaned in. "Let me ask you something, Madison. If Alex lost everything tomorrow, would you stay with him?"

Madison's nod was immediate and unequivocal, though the question lingered in her mind. Could Alex lose everything? It was difficult to imagine, but in this day and age, anything was possible.

"I think, no matter what, I'll always be here for him. It's hard to explain, but with Alex, I feel a connection. It's something I can't deny and I can't explain. It's just there." Madison smothered a light laugh, but freely smiled. "I feel silly saying it because our relationship is so new. And there are still so many things I don't know about him."

Averting her gaze, Jess took an extra-long sip of wine.

Madison had a feeling Jess knew more than she'd ever say. She seemed loyal that way.

Finally, Jess said, "Alex has had his shields up a long time. It's hard living a life where you're not always sure who you can trust. But he trusts you, Madison, which is maybe the biggest step I've ever seen the man take. He might be a kickass CEO to the rest of the world, but I think in your hands, he's pretty much putty."

Jess's words made Madison smile. Her gaze dropped, and she noticed a small framed photo next to the wine bottle. Looking closer, she realized it was their men posing in front of the Statue of Liberty, younger versions of themselves.

"So, how about Alex and Mark," she asked. "How did they meet?"

Jess set down her wineglass and stood, her light expression taking on a more somber look. She turned away, taking a few deliberate steps to the mammoth stone fireplace. With the long arm of the poker, she pushed at the logs, losing herself in the spark and roar of the flames. Whatever secrets she was harboring seemed to be well guarded, as if they weren't hers to share.

Eventually, she returned the poker to its wrought-iron caddy and turned back, keeping her response vague. "Oh, they've known each other for years. Like brothers. They can tell you more over dinner, but they've leaned on each other time and time again. In their circle, trust is a priceless commodity, and the trust they have in each other is limitless. There's nothing they wouldn't do for each other. Speaking of trust, are you ready for tomorrow?"

Madison recalled the conversation she and Alex had in the

helicopter before they arrived. He'd arranged an activity for them tomorrow, something she'd never tried before. The lump that rose in her throat at the thought of it could only be forced down with a large swallow of cab.

"As ready as I'm going to be, I guess."

Can anyone really be ready for this?

Anxiety had been Madison's steady companion for many years, as constant and normal as eating, sleeping, and breathing, sticking to her like her shadow.

But the nervous energy she had for what was to come was different—a raw mix of fear and thrill, reinforced with a strong dose of faith that knew no bounds but had no beginning. Faith that this unconventional idea would be worth a try. Faith that thirty days with Alex would be worth a try.

Even a decade later, the wave of hurt that shattered her over and over again at the memory of her brother, Jack—the loss never failed to leave her numb, but she always managed to paste on a smile and tackle another endless day. Numbness was good. Isolation was better. But being with Alex was like pure oxygen, giving her one easy breath after another.

Like so many things in Madison's life, Alex somehow seemed to sense and understood her grief and anxiety. Was that why it was easy? Because he could see past her well-practiced facade?

They never discussed it. She never let him in. So, how did he know? How could he possibly know to ask her how she was coping? *Coping,* he'd said. Not coped. Not the past-tense presumption everyone else used.

And Alex Drake saw everything. The indiscernible shrug she would give in response that should have moved his questions along. The avoiding glance to hide the burning tears in her eyes. The soft shudder of her breath that did all it could to stave off the inevitable breakdown.

It was enough for Alex to see her agony. See it and offer her a different way out, an alternative to fighting her feelings—to take on the domination of each raw emotion head-on. To push past everything she'd fooled herself into thinking she controlled, and finally let go.

That was what tomorrow's activity could give her, Alex had promised, and she was both terrified and eager to give it a whirl.

Jess reached over to pat Madison's arm. "Don't worry about it. You're in terrific hands. Alex actually taught me and Mark. He'll earn your trust."

I believe you.

When the boys barged in wearing the widest grins and outlandish chef's hats as they announced dinner was served, each woman headed to her man.

As they made their way past the kitchen, with each square inch of gourmet countertop pristine despite the frenzy of cooking going on not long ago, Madison couldn't help but beam at two titans of industry being so handy in the kitchen.

Alex led her past an eat-in seating area that offered no food at all, and out to an oversize deck overflowing with candles and flowers. There, they'd arranged a spread with so much food, the two couples would have to nibble on it for the entire long weekend just to make a dent.

The flickering candles reached high, snapping up the last beams of sunlight that were quickly simmering behind the lake. Taking a seat, Madison accepted the peck Alex placed on her cheek, and continued reconciling Alex Drake, masterful CEO, with Alex Drake, the man.

Jess discreetly pointed out the men's matching kiss the chef aprons, as if they could be missed, and leaned over to whisper, "You thinking what I'm thinking?"

Madison lifted her wineglass and tapped it gently to Jess's. "That we're staring at dessert?"

"*Bon appétit*," she said with hints of an Adirondack accent and a resonating clink.

"So, are you ready for tomorrow?" Mark asked Madison, and

when she nodded meekly, he gave her a reassuring wink. "You know, Alex Drake might look the part of a titan of industry and world-renounced CEO, but he's also managed to convince me that this, how shall we put it, *unconventional method* can help."

"Hey, I only said it helped me," he said, modest in his admission.

"There we were," Mark continued, "a ragtag group of vets desperate to dig ourselves out from being explosive, or reactive, or desolate, or numb. We didn't want much. Just a single freaking day without anguish would be nice."

Alex shrugged. "Back then, the concept was new. A way to deal with PTSD that didn't have to do with sharing your feelings."

"We're guys," Mark added. "No one ever accused us of being in touch with our feelings. But the beauty of this was that a bunch of macho guys could get behind it. Everyone who heard about it was all in."

"Family members were all in too. And this wasn't a 'treatment.' No one was there to analyze reactions or keep count. This was a lifeline of hope for people at their wits' end." Alex beamed. It was the first time since she'd known him that she detected unapologetic pride.

Mark patted him on the back. "For some of us, it was something . . . sometimes the only thing . . . we could look forward to in order to feel normal. For others, it brought calm, peace of mind, and solace."

"Does it do that for you?" Madison asked gently.

Thoughtfully, he replied. "For the first time in a long time, it gave me purpose. A purpose I needed. Help others. Give back. Make a difference. Save people where I ... I missed the chance before." He took a large sip of wine before Madison pressed a kiss to his lips.

"I'll get us some cappuccino," Mark said.

"I'll help." Jess and Mark rushed to the kitchen as Alex fed her a fresh strawberry.

The deck was softly lit by torches, but it was what was beyond it that captured Madison's attention between easy chatter about each of their lives and the sinful bites of delicious food. As darkness closed in, Madison could still see the woods just beyond the lake, and wondered if this was the reason they all loved it here. It was more than a tranquil paradise where nature harmonized with the people in it.

It was private. Secluded. No one made pretenses, and everyone settled comfortably into the contentment of just being themselves. In a world of power players and corporate climbers, Madison was a nobody. But here, she breathed easier, knowing that even a nobody would be welcomed, just being herself.

Alex's warm hand wrapped around hers, pulling her back from the distance her mind drifted off to. His smile was contagious, and she gave him a wider one in return.

Madison relished the intimate glances they shared. The hidden moments where the world vanished and nothing existed but them. Those intimate seconds that wove them together with each passing day were everything, where she could learn more about the reclusive man, and settle into the comfort of the two of them growing even closer.

CHAPTER 9

ALEX

That evening, Alex stood on the balcony off the guest room wearing only his warm flannel pajama bottoms, splitting the set and leaving the top for Madison. It had become a comfortable routine back at his place.

Back home.

Here at Mark and Jess's, which had become his home away from home over the years, the decor was rustic and woodsy, with modern wood beams and stone accents throughout. Expansive glass paneling wrapped around the balcony, providing a seamless view of the evergreen forest in the distance.

With the sliding doors set invisibly past the edges of the wall, there was no divide between the heated room and the chilly outdoors. The fresh air would float through the room and then swirl back out, wafts of warm and cool air softly skimming the bare skin of his chest and back.

The setting was serene, but Alex could feel the strain of his knuckles, growing whiter with each passing minute of clutching the rail for dear life.

Sporadic tiny bursts from fireflies blinked against the darkness of the pines, giving him too little to focus on. So he stared off, concentrating on pulling in each breath. The tug-of-war with his body was a fight—one he battled nightly to win.

Not now, he insisted to himself again and again. *Not now.* Deep breath in. *Not now.* Slow breath out. Each breath was ragged but he pressed on, barely controlling the erratic spikes of his runaway pulse.

Even when the sweat streaming down his forehead, neck, and back burned like ice, Alex remained still. Calm. The episodes passed faster that way, when he focused and didn't move.

The relentless thumping of his own heart in his ears always deafened him, which he turned into a game. Counting the beats kept him sane. As if ticking off the days in his body's prison, he waited out the wave without losing his remaining sanity.

It will pass. It has to.

Shattering his focus, a sudden high-pitched mechanical squeal broke through the silence, which always happened when the guest shower hadn't been used for months. The sound was annoying as shit. But tonight, it was his saving grace, alerting him that he had a little more time to get himself under control.

Madison can't see me like this.

Desperate, he picked up his cell phone and punched at the same number over and over again, barely waiting for it to be sent to voice mail before swearing under his breath and trying again. "Goddammit. Pick up, Mark. Fuck."

Frustrated, he hurled his phone as far out into the darkness as he could. Gripping the handrail again, Alex closed his eyes as he focused, focused, focused.

On Madison.

The softness of her long wavy hair when she'd first wake up. The fullness of her lips when they pressed against his. The sparkle that lit her eyes every time she saw him, and the smile that always followed. She was the first woman he'd brought up here. She'd caught on to that. Did she know she was the first woman to move in with him? The only woman? With Madison, everything felt right.

Yes. Madison.

He sucked in an even deeper breath, filling his lungs and holding it. Slowly, the tremors that racked his body finally subsided.

Her footsteps were light, but he could gauge her distance behind him. When her hands slid around the tension in his torso and her cheek rested against his bare back, he released his breath in a long, slow exhale.

Opening his eyes, he noticed the darkness of the tree line twinkling with distant fireflies again. Her warm lips pressed against his back, and his heart rate slowed from its unbearable high of just seconds ago.

A last labored breath was all he needed—giving him an extra moment before facing her.

CHAPTER 10

MADISON

Madison emerged from the bathroom, greeted by the sweet scent of fresh air blending with the hickory logs ablaze in the fireplace. The flannel top was right where she expected it, waiting for her on the corner of the bed, just like at Alex's place.

Back home.

She pressed the snuggly soft fabric to her nose and inhaled the familiar smell of cedar, wondering how many times Alex had worn these pajamas here at the cabin over the years.

Her breath hitched, as it always did whenever she saw him. He stood tall against the backdrop of twilight, every muscle in his solid back ripped and carved, drawing her in and lighting a desire so strong, she could never hold back.

Needing him was more than anything physical, though an outsider looking in might not know it. In this moment, he was distant, carried far away in his own thoughts. She'd give anything for a peek into whatever was pulling him far from here. From her.

Something was bothering him. Feverishly, he seemed to be attacking his phone with his thumb, impatient and muttering.

Shocked, Madison watched him heave the phone out into the darkness.

Frowning with confusion, she said nothing, because what was there to say? *Are you all right?*

It was the same question that made her cringe when people asked, making her want to bare her teeth at them. *Sure. I'm fine. Barely able to eat, sleep, or breathe, but everything's hunky-dory. Move along . . . nothing to see here, folks. Nope, nothing to see.*

Maybe she and Alex were alike in that way. Maybe not. It didn't matter. In that moment, Madison had two choices. Run . . . or stay.

In a few quiet steps, Madison closed in, skimming her fingers across the small of his back, then smoothing her hands around to the flat of his sculpted abs. Securing her hold around his waist, she pressed her cheek to his back before placing a tender kiss to his skin.

With her arms wrapped around him, his thundering heartbeat slowed and his quick breaths leveled off. As did hers.

Though his hand covered hers, he barely turned his head, taking an unusual pause before speaking. "Hey, if you have any reservations about tomorrow, it's okay. No pressure."

No pressure. And we aren't going to talk about what's upsetting him, because "no pressure."

"No," she said slowly, "I want to do it. From what you've said, it might help me sort a few things out. Issues I've had problems dealing with."

Madison hesitated to talk more about her quest through self-exploration. Burdening others seemed like a chore more than a relief. The last thing people needed to know about was her personal hell of anxiety and panic attacks fueled by loss and pain.

"Let's do something," he said.

Alex turned and moved inside for a moment to pick up a small ottoman. His smile was comforting, but she wondered why he'd bring it out to the balcony's edge.

"Here." He grabbed her hand, urging her to stand on it. Then, with some unspoken plan, his hands firmed around her hips, turning her to face the woods.

The railing was tall, but only met her at the kneecap. She took a nervous look down, balancing on one foot and then another before easing into the confidence she was safe. Alex's hands lingered on her hips, reinforcing her position.

"Did you ever see *Titanic*?"

"With Leo and Kate?" she asked with a casual familiarity as if I knew the megastars personally.

"Remember the scene where they were on the bow of the ship? She stretched her arms way out, embracing the air and the sensation of being one with everything around her. The sunset. The ocean. Having faith in everything in the moment."

"She had faith in him," Madison said. If there was one thing she loved, it was a great love story.

Pulling in a breath, she played out the scene, taking all her lessons from high school drama to the next level. She stretched her arms wide, looking out into the darkness with vivid recollections of the orange-and-blue sky in the scene. The ship as it sailed across an endless sea. The breathless moment of that amazing onscreen kiss.

With strength and intention, Alex leaned her body forward, giving her the smallest taste of how it might feel. "This is what you'll do tomorrow. Just think of that scene, and you'll be fine."

His hold on her hips tugged her back until she stood tall again on the ottoman. Both of his hands moved ever so slightly higher, slowly inching up the hem of the soft shirt and baring her ass.

Madison's giggle was instant. "My view is spectacular. How's yours?" She shot him a playful glance over her shoulder.

"Getting better and better." His murmurs of approval deepened as a breeze swept across the bare skin of her butt.

"Is there anything I can do to help?"

Without warning, he yanked her back, letting her willing body fall into the cradle of his arms. "I can think of a few things."

His mouth met hers with a tenderness that pried her lips open, urging her to take the smallest tip of his tongue as he stole a taste. The next sweep was rushed and hungrier than the first. The feel of his searing lips as they molded with hers sent electricity everywhere, lighting a wildfire throughout her body.

With a few steps into the room, he spread her across a plush rug close to the logs roaring in the stone fireplace. Soft pillows and blankets had been scattered near the hearth, making the rustic space feel romantic and sensual.

As Alex joined Madison, she skimmed her fingers over his skin. Fascinated, she explored every line and curve of his shoulders and chest, while his hand slid across the sensitive plane of her inner thigh.

His hand moved in a slow path to the fullness of her ass before pulling her in, taunting her aching pussy with the heat of his flannel-encased erection pressing hard to her core.

With each button of her shirt he tugged away, he explored another new area of exposed skin with his lips, nibbling across her breasts, then up her neck. Her shirt was open and undone when he asked, "How's this for camping?" His warm whisper didn't linger at her ear, and his hot kisses quickly trailed down.

"Oh, it'll be perfect in a while."

Mid-kiss, he stopped. Amused, he pinned her with a playful glare.

"And just what, Ms. Taylor, would make it more perfect?" he grumbled, tracing a long line across her collarbone, between her breasts, then nearly to her wetness before pulling his sinful finger back. Opening her shirt, Alex exposed one breast at a time, then stroked her peaked nipples lightly with his tongue. "Hmm?"

The bite to her own lip didn't help getting her words out. With heavier breaths, Madison tried again. "Well, uh, usually when people camp, it's beneath a big, open sky."

"Interesting," he murmured across her neck. "Did you want to go outside?" This time, he let the tip of his teeth graze her nipple before he lapped it with a heated lick.

"N-no. But, uh, this will all be perfect as soon as you have me seeing stars." She moaned, arching her back as he popped her full breast into his mouth, suckling her as she began a slow ride against the strength of his thigh.

"I'll do my best," Alex said, working his fingers along the wetness weeping from her folds.

When he swiped his wet fingers across her clit, she moved in harmony with his hand, taking in every circle—every blissful sensation—across her desperate bundle of nerves.

"I need you," she whispered, running her fingernails tenderly across the skin of his neck as she begged.

He removed his pants, letting her see the thick fullness of his dick, its tip glistening. "I'm yours, Madison," he murmured against her lips.

She watched as he moved to retrieve a condom, not bothering to tear it open or put it on. Not yet. His was a body to be admired, and admire it she did, losing herself in every sculpted muscle. Eventually, she pulled her gaze away from his abs and chest to finally meet his eyes.

Kneeling, he took her in, his dark, hungry gaze holding more than heat and desire. Beyond, she could see the longing. Like he'd never had her before. As if she'd never been his.

She gave him a tender smile, hoping every worry and doubt between them could disappear. *I will always be yours, Alex Drake.*

He remained still, patiently allowing her to drink him in with her eyes. And her journey along the dips and valleys of his body was unrushed. Alex Drake was a work of art. Etched to perfection. Strong, yet vulnerable. Willing to let her in, but not weak.

She understood how precious a gift was his trust. He was the epitome of power, yet he'd relinquished all of it to her mercy. Giving himself over. Being truly exposed.

In return, her desire for him was unyielding. She wanted to be anything and everything he needed. Be completely his.

But of all the emotions swirling within her now, the one taking over was lust.

With a suggestive lick across the fullness of her lip, she slipped her hand through his inner thighs, tugging his body forward to her eager, waiting lips. The drop on his tip needed a long lick before he forced himself through to the back of her throat.

"Yes, Madison." He dropped his head back, a low rumble leaving his throat. His fingers wove through the thickness of her hair until her position and pace mirrored his wants. Just the rhythm made her wet.

Alex's movements were masterful, controlled, as he turned her on her back, keeping his throbbing cock in her mouth. She gasped with anticipation as his head made its way to the throbbing between her legs.

The first lick made her shiver. The second made her hips rock and sway, as every touch between her legs had her climbing. Chasing. Keeping the rhythm of her mouth closely matched to his, and fighting every impulse that pounded her swollen pussy.

Because coming was not an option. Not yet.

When his mouth devoured her clit, her submission was imminent. Their bodies intertwined, locking in the depths of their erotic feeding. The lashes of his tongue were amplified as his fingers smeared across her—rubbed her—invaded her.

And with increased pace, Madison stroked and sucked, taking him deeper while tenderly teasing the sensitive skin of his sac.

The taste of Alex was stronger as he forced himself further in. And the fingers he slid through her swollen folds were too much, hitting the one spot that could always make her shatter at his whim.

She tried to match his pace, but it was elusive. His tongue

focused on her pulsing clit, and his relentless fingers strummed her spot, coaxing her orgasm ahead of his own.

Uncontrolled, her climax ripped a cry from her mouth, pulling her from his bulging cock with a gasp. Her throaty screams filled the air, while she rode his face and fingers through her ecstasy.

"Are you seeing stars yet?" he growled naughtily, still enjoying licking the swollen lips of her soaked pussy, while keeping his fingers firmly in place.

"Yes," she cried at the top of her lungs. "Yes. Yes."

Her eyelids fluttered, opening enough for her to realize the balcony door was open and had been . . . *the entire time*.

"Oh my God, I didn't mean to be so loud." Madison panted, breathless and embarrassed, wondering what Jess and Mark must be thinking.

With a final swipe along her walls, Alex had her back arching and legs trembling as he pulled his fingers from her. Her body writhed from the loss. As he kissed his way back to her face, she couldn't help but draw him in, aroused as her lips tasted the fresh dew of her own essence.

"Well, they're about to hear a whole lot more," he said low.

Condom in hand, he slid the sheath on. With more control than any man should have, Alex glided the head of his rigid cock in and out, teasing her folds before plunging it to the hilt.

Again, her whimpers kicked up to screams. "Yes. God, yes."

With a steady pace, his lips plucked at a nipple, letting it snap back from a light tug of his teeth.

"I'm close," Madison murmured. "So close . . ." Her body moved with his, needy for every sensation. Every touch.

Alex's pace quickened and his thrusts became rougher. Harder. Deeper. And she couldn't hold back.

Her eyes fluttered and her back arched. "Please. I—I have to come again."

"God, yes," he said, filling her, pounding her, taking her to the brink with circle after circle along her clit.

Both tumbled deep into the erotic abyss, riding each other's waves and crying out as loud as their bodies would let them. Each sensual movement was ecstasy. Then his hot release erupted in a series of heavy thrusts that threatened to tear them both apart.

After their heaving breaths slowed and their bodies cooled, Alex slipped away for a moment, returning with a thicker blanket for Madison, though he seemed to prefer the gentle breeze, comforted in the swaddle of the fresh night air. He slipped a pillow gently beneath Madison's head before taking one for himself, keeping a loving watch on her as she peered at him through eyes heavy with satisfaction.

Wincing, she whispered, "I'm positive they heard us." Giggling, she pulled the blanket up over her face, hiding the heat blazing across her cheeks.

Undeterred, Alex tugged the bedding, pulling it down. "Beautiful, I'm sure the penguins in Antarctica heard us."

His playful laugh ended in another kiss on her lips. Nuzzling into the warmth of his chest, Madison gazed at the fireplace with its bright sparks and dancing flames as her mind drifted.

A few words floated up from her subconscious, often silent but always there. She shoved them down, avoiding the wonder of Alex—or at least, avoiding it for now. Carried off to an exhausted sleep, she only faintly heard the thought now.

Who is Alex Drake?

CHAPTER 11

MADISON

Madison couldn't recall exactly when or how she moved from the floor, but there she was, snug in the plush, oversize bed, enjoying the sunlight that warmed her skin as she yawned. With a glance around and no sounds from the bathroom, she realized Alex had to be gone.

And not just gone. All traces of their campground escapade had been magically erased. Even the fireplace seemed undisturbed, cool and untouched.

Did I dream it?

She lifted the covers and took a good look at herself. Though Alex's flannel pajama shirt still wrapped her arms, it didn't cover much else, remaining unbuttoned and open.

Nope. Not a dream.

A huge smile stretched her cheeks as thoughts of his stubble wreaking havoc on the insides of her legs played back. With a stretch, she revisited her afterglow until a few knocks interrupted her luscious jaunt down memory lane and her own hand massaging her thigh.

"Madison, you up?"

Surprised, Madison froze for a second before her fingers

worked feverishly, refastening one button after the other. Realizing her frazzled work ended in a total misalignment of the two sides, she abandoned working on her clothes and pulled the comforter high.

"Come on in, Jess."

Bright as a spring daisy, Jess strolled in with two mugs of coffee in hand. How her bed head and flannel robe managed to make her look like a pinup, Madison would never know.

"Morning," Jess said with only the slightest yawn. "Alex said you might like a little coffee."

"Mmm, yes, please." Madison leaned over for a long stretch, receiving the steaming mug with eager hands.

Like long-time friends, Jess plopped on the bed next to her, taking a refreshing sip from her own cup. "So, Julia Child and Betty Crocker are rustling us up some breakfast, but be warned. Those boys can really cook. Everything you see will look amazing, but don't eat more than a bite."

"Why not?"

"For what you're doing today, you'll be walking a fine line between eating enough to have something in your tummy and overfilling the tank—risking a mid-event upchuck."

"Toast and bacon it is." Madison nodded, already battling bouts of queasiness whenever she thought about the day ahead. The last thing she needed was that sort of lasting impression.

"Breakfast should be ready in about fifteen minutes," Jess said with a few light pats on Madison's knee through the overfilled comforter. With her coffee in hand, she headed for the door.

"Um, Jess, before you go." *I have to know.* "Did you and Mark hear anything last night?" Nervous about the response, Madison winced as she held her breath.

"Hear anything?" Jess's pursed lips and uncertain glance revealed nothing. "I'm not sure. What would it have sounded like?"

The cries of *oh God* and *yes, please, yes* looped through Madison's mind as her answer stalled. "Oh, I don't know, just, you know . . . anything. Anything out of the ordinary."

"Well, we usually sleep like logs, so we don't hear much. But last night? What were we doing? Oh, we were too wrapped up in a ton of hot, sweaty sex to hear a thing."

Madison relaxed, giggling.

"What can I say?" Jess said with a wink before she headed out. "I'm a screamer."

∽

This was it, the moment of truth.

Madison couldn't quite believe what they were doing. What she was doing. The toast and bacon had plenty of time to settle, but instead, they did flips in her belly, sending sweat to her hands and wild pulses to her heart.

I don't know if I can do this.

The emotions racing through her were fickle, shifting from *daredevil thrill* one minute, to *freaked out and ready to call it quits* the next. Then to *hell yeah.* Then to being worried she'd pee her pants.

Between her thundering heartbeat and near hyperventilation, Madison focused on what was needed most. Controlling her bladder.

If I ever do this again, the second cup of coffee is a hard pass!

Alex took his position behind her, though he felt a million miles away as he shouted, "You okay?"

Convincingly, Madison nodded and then held up her thumb.

His voice loud, Alex kept her motivated. "Just do what I told you. If you don't get there, it's no big deal. But I'm ready when you are."

Keep calm. Big breath in. *I can do this.* Slow breath out.

Madison's mind quieted, and the wind in her face gave her the strangest sense of peace. For the moment, that was a good thing.

Alex's lessons had been gentle, reminding her that reactions are personal. One person might laugh. Another might cry. Some had even ended their session in gut-wrenching screams. Or jubilant shouts. Maybe all of the above. Maybe none of these at all. Anything was possible. And everyone was right.

"We feel what we feel," were his words, and Madison knew he was bracing her. Preparing her for some lack of control that wouldn't be shamed and shouldn't be held in. "Just . . . let it all out. It'll help you let go."

This was the Alex she had to know. The man who helped others without any kind of spotlight. Founding a group dedicated to helping as many as he could, most of them vets.

Embracing the moment, Madison closed her eyes and did as they'd rehearsed, the scene on the bow of the ship in *Titanic*. Throwing her arms wide, she summoned the courage to open her eyes and let it all go. Control. Fear. Doubt.

The goggles she wore gave her a bird's eye view of everything, including her life. A life that was meant for more than wading through the weighty sludge of pain. One that needed to be lived.

Pushing past the tightness in her chest, she leaned forward. Took a step. And fell.

It was faster than she could have imagined, and she panicked at first, then plummeted with terrifying elation and abandon. Freefalling ten thousand feet was one hell of a way to let everything go. And away they went, falling to the earth at a dizzying speed without a care.

She'd nearly forgotten Alex until his body shifted and tightened against her. As it was in all areas of their relationship, Alex Drake had her back, one tandem leap at a time.

Skydiving was a rush she couldn't understand. Madison didn't shout or laugh. The only clue she gave Alex that she was conscious and hadn't fainted was that her arms remained rigid, flying free from her sides.

Awestruck, she took in every sensation, imagining herself, not so much in gravity's hold, but more in a spirited freedom of flight. *A hundred twenty-two miles per second*, she recounted in wild disbelief.

"Ready?" Alex said, shouting.

Nodding, she pulled her arms in, wrapping her hands tight to the straps of her harness. The surge of adrenaline that followed pervaded every cell of her body.

I've got this. I'm ready.

Alex took the lead and deployed the drogue parachute. It was the beginning of the end, reducing their speed while prolonging the sensation of the freefall.

A pop sounded as the final larger chute deployed, jerking them up gently before slowing them with its drag. Alex grabbed the toggles, easily steering them with strength and skill. The dizzying freefall descent was slower now as they glided to the open field—the drop zone. Jess's little body waved up at them, and the picturesque field grew closer by the second.

As the ground closed in, Madison prepared. In front tandem form, she lifted her legs, stretching them in front of her, so Alex could take the lead in landing them.

Gliding into the lush, green grass, the landing reminded Madison of a slip-and-slide, zooming freely to the end. She knew Alex would have both knees bent, taking the brunt of the force as he dragged them to a gentle stop.

Falling back, Madison could feel her cheeks draw into a wide smile, but her exhilaration faded quickly, disrupted by a few tears that gathered in the rim of her goggles.

Jess was ready, running over to them to help collect the parachute as Alex unclipped it and removed his harness. His goggles off, he gave Madison a concerned glance.

She couldn't move. Or speak. Or understand anything that was happening.

Instead, she just rested against him, letting him remove her goggles and untether her from the harness. His thumbs gently whisked away her runaway tears, letting her come to terms with her confusing emotions in her own time.

Checking in, he asked, "How do you feel?"

Madison couldn't control the creases in her brow, but she could feel them. Her emotions tumbled over each other, moment by moment, shifting their weight from one feeling to the next.

It's too much.

Her body felt lifeless. Heavy and weak. Alex stroked her arm, but she could see he was studying her.

I don't want him to worry.

She tried a small movement, but he held her in place.

"It's all right," he said low. "Stay still. I'll be right back." Gently, he rolled her body off his and laid her down on the grass.

Madison watched as he moved over to Jess and asked softly for a blanket. Saying how they'd enjoy some time alone for a bit, but that two bottles of water would be appreciated.

Alex was again by her side, and the bottles of water appeared, though she didn't recall seeing Jess. Lifting Madison's head, he offered her a sip.

Swallowing, she looked away, ashamed that more tears were escaping. "I'm sor—"

"Hey," he said, sitting beside her and taking care to wipe the tears from her face. "You're fine. We don't have to talk, remember? We feel what we feel. And we can stay here as long as you like."

Madison again hadn't noticed Jess until she felt the warmth of the cashmere throw on her shoulders. Before Madison could thank her, Jess was gone.

Tucking the lightweight blanket around her and up to her chin, Alex seemed content to stay lovingly away. With an insistent pull, she drew his body closer to hers. To lie beside her.

"I'm not going anywhere," he said, laying tender kisses along her cheek. "We have all the time in the world, Madison Taylor. I'll always be by your side."

A comment like that might have garnered a reaction an hour ago. But not now.

With the sun shining and birds chirping, she knew she needed to snap out of it, hop up, and enjoy the day. But she was paralyzed, lost in a journey that wouldn't be done until every last emotion was acknowledged and assessed until it faded away.

So, she lay there, weeping with this remarkable man, losing herself in the changing shapes and colors of the clouds high up in the sky.

CHAPTER 12

MADISON

Midway through her first morning back at work, Madison's messenger window popped up with a welcome message. Not from Alex, but welcome, nonetheless. Alex's right-hand man, Paco Robles, had quickly become her bestie. It was only then that she realized she hadn't seen him in over a week.

> *Paco: Hey, a good girl like you wouldn't happen to know anyone who plays poker and doesn't mind healthy stakes?*

The twenty seconds she waited before replying was the best she could do at a virtual poker face.

> *Madison: My poker's not terrible, though it's been a while. Got a game?*

> *Paco: Yes! Lost our fourth to love and marriage. If you're good for Wednesday evenings, I'll add you to our group.*

She checked the calendar.

Madison: Tonight's Wednesday.

Paco: Exactly. Game day. We'll have your induction ceremony tonight.

Madison: What's the buy-in?

Paco: Normally $1000. Alex has a tab.

Madison: I'm good. My piggy bank is all kinds of plump at the moment. And it'll be fatter after tonight.

Paco: Game on, girlie!

Madison: See you there.

Fired up, she rubbed her hands together, prepared to count her winnings.

It's totally in the bag.

∼

As the valet rushed to open Madison's door, she sprang from her Lyft with a shy *thanks*. Taking in the magnificence of the Carlyle Hotel, she found the iconic building brimming with elegance and history, and right in the heart of Manhattan's Upper East Side. One glance up, and the fancy skyscraper seemed to be barely a tiptoe from touching the sky.

Though another man held open a side door, Madison politely declined, opting for a fun spin through the revolving door. She landed just inside, surrounded by the Old World grace of stately potted palms, black marble floors, and crystal chandeliers.

After another glance at the cryptic text from Paco, she headed to the concierge.

Paco: Ten paces to the concierge desk.

I think he forgot a step.

With the concierge at the desk already giving her a helpful smile, Madison strolled over. "Hi. I'm not sure—"

"Good evening, Ms. Taylor. I believe this is for you."

As he handed over a deep red envelope, Madison smiled. Her name was scrolled across it with a smiley face in the *o*.

"Thank you," she said.

"My pleasure. Is there anything more I can do for you?"

Madison shook her head, satisfied for the moment with the mystery of a note. Inside the envelope was a card, but no key. On the fancy Carlyle stationery, the handwritten note held seven smart-ass words.

Don't lose your money too fast, Taylor.

She flipped the card over, noticing the bold strokes that gave the brief instructions a sense of suspense and intrigue.

Private Elevator.
Penthouse.

Penthouse? Of course.

Madison headed toward the elevator, taking her time to study the paintings lining several walls. As she reached it, she realized she wouldn't be alone in the car. This elevator had an operator, just as it had fifty years before. Like the concierge before him, he knew exactly where she was going.

When the elevator stopped, it opened to a lavish suite of magnificent scale, with high ceilings that showed off every inch of rich wallpapered and wainscoted areas, brocade drapes, and exotic rugs. Each piece of furniture perfectly offset the opulent architecture, and still preserved a coziness. A warmth.

"Hello?" Madison called out as she took a few careful steps in.

"Well, here's a hustler if I've ever seen one . . . and not in the prostitution way."

Silver-tongued and as suave as ever, Paco entered, looking as elegant as his surroundings. Daringly, he wore his satin smoking jacket *sans* shirt, its pattern a rich peacock-colored paisley that only he could pull off. Taking in his black satin pants and gold smoking slippers, Madison imagined this was as dressed down as the man got shy of being buck-ass naked.

Noting the two pink cocktails he carried, Madison reconsidered his outfit. *If this turns into a strip poker game, I'm out of here.*

"Thanks for inviting me," she said, and they exchanged a light kiss on the cheek.

"Hey, Madison, glad you could join us," Ted said as he and Rex walked in, enjoying their own bottles of beer.

The dynamic duo of DGI's IT division were often referred to collectively as TRex due to their strangely similar appearances, even though they had to be ten years apart in age.

"Paco's been great about letting us use his place for our weekly game," Ted said with another sip.

"It's stunning," Madison said, admiring it again.

"Thanks. Grey Goose cosmo?" Paco asked.

Graciously, she accepted, determined to pace herself. But after her first sip and an exaggerated *mmm*, she sipped again. *Okay, pacing myself is crazy talk.*

"What's in the bottom," she asked.

"Two Griottines cherries, because I had a feeling you'd like it extra sweet," Paco said with a smile.

"Okay, but you're not allowed to use your infamous mind-reading during the game." Madison held up her champagne coupe for a toast, solidifying their new card-sharp camaraderie.

Paco clinked with his twin cosmo, and TRex brought their beers in. She took another sip of the recently poured drink, fresh with itsy-bitsy ice chips still floating at the top. The refreshing and energizing imbibement was just what she needed to relax.

"Before we go to the card room . . ." *Because, of course, a place like this has a card room.* "You have a little something to remove, Miss Madison," Paco said rather insistently.

Since she'd first taken in his chiseled abs showcased in the elegant smoking jacket open clear to his navel, Madison had loosely considered a convenient exit strategy in the event this did turn out to be a strip-poker game. Just in case. Mentally flipping through several alternatives, she settled for the old standby, *a sudden case of diarrhea*, to quickly excuse herself.

Looking anxiously around for the nearest bathroom, and on the brink of asking, she noticed Paco's not so subtle glances down. Her gaze quizzically followed his to her own feet. Then to his. Then to the delightful feet of the dynamic duo.

Smoking slippers. They were all wearing gold smoking slippers, each with their initials embroidered on top.

A burst of relieved laughter left her lips. Well, relief coupled with amusement at seeing Ted and Rex's matching ensembles paired with such elegant slippers. They'd managed to carry off hiker-meets-NASA engineer, topped off by the royal family.

The fun of kicking off her heels and sliding each foot into these pillows of heaven was only made better by admiring her own monograms in the top. *Best princess poker tournament ever.*

Paco led them to a room filled with golden art deco accents, red wallpaper, and black drapes, obviously decorated by the Queen of Hearts himself. The octagonal felt-lined card table was ready, with small side tables for each player brimming with charcuterie, berries, finger pastries, and an area for each of their drinks.

Paco took his seat opposite from Madison, and Ted and Rex naturally fell into place on each side of her. Paco's hands were a whirl as he manipulated the cards, flipping them between shuffles, and showing off in a way that seemed purely for Madison's delight. She watched, fascinated by the magician who could pull her smile from thin air.

Finally, he dealt. "Five-card draw. Nothing wild. Ante up."

As everyone tossed a few chips into the center of the table, Rex leaned over to Madison. "And if you lose all your money, you still get to play."

"I love it. How long do you play for?" she asked.

"Until Ted starts his usual string of incessant yawns. A few hours at most," Paco teased.

CHAPTER 13

PACO

After a few rounds of drawing, calling, and folding, an uneasy and slightly irritated feeling crept over Paco. His poker Spidey sense, that uneasy feeling of being played, was in full swing.

"Madison, did I hear you're the maid of honor at a wedding?" Ted asked. "That sounds fun."

"Well, yes. I just need a date."

Paco coughed up his sip of cosmo, practically choking it out his nose. Rex leaned over to lay several hard pats on his back. Determined, Paco grunted his breathing into submission, trying not to fly off the handle.

"Why don't you have a date?" he said sharply, his indignation coming off a little stronger than intended. "I thought you *were* seeing someone."

"Well, yes, I am." Madison's feeble attempt at calm and collected didn't exactly soothe his alarm. "I am definitely seeing *someone*. But, well, I'm just not sure we're ready to take things to the next level."

"The next level?" he asked, giving her a blank look.

"Mm-hmm. You know. We haven't exactly decided to go . . . public."

EXPOSED

"We? So, it's a joint decision? As in both of you." Paco held his cards high, intentionally covering most of his subdued, pissed-off expression, though there was no masking his paternal tone of disapproval.

Madison's already covering for Alex and his pervasive asshole streak. What the fuck is wrong with him? I am so going to kick his ass.

Studying her, Paco didn't miss much as she sank lower in her seat and started fidgeting with her arm. *Shit. I'm triggering her hives.* Paco figured he had about ten seconds to make it right before Madison bolted with some lame excuse.

I'd bet a c-note she'll go for the old daring diarrhea escape.

He'd deal with his own feelings later, likely with a size twelve shoe up Alex's ass. For now, he'd seduce her with, of all things, an obvious mistake. He'd paid attention, round after round. Madison Taylor was a cunning little card counter. Just like him. Except, she used her superpowers to lose.

With renewed energy, Paco shuffled and dealt a fresh hand. It took about half a second for Ted and Rex to fold.

"Raise," Paco said, smiling confidently at Madison. He raised a brow, showcasing his most charming dimples, double-daring her to play.

"Raise, huh?" Madison let out a laugh.

He knew it, and it was written all over her face that she knew it too. His hand was pure shit.

"Just to be crystal clear," she said smugly, "you said raise?"

"Yeah, girl. I said raise." He defiantly polished off his drink, then flipped his glass, forcing the cherry to fly through the air and land squarely in his mouth. He chomped it, channeling a smart-ass schoolgirl popping gum.

"Oh, challenge accepted." Madison pushed her chips forward, mimicking Paco's suave demeanor, and finished off her own drink.

But as she attempted the final move, flipping the glass to toss the cherry into the air, she overshot, forgetting there were two.

Flying high, one cherry landed squarely in her wide-open mouth, but the other took an Olympic dive straight down her blouse, lodging securely in its new nesting spot deep between her breasts.

Wide-eyed, she scanned the room as if hoping no one had noticed. As usual, the TRex twins played it as cool as Paco imagined they could. Ted kept his stare on the felted table, studying it intently. Meanwhile, Rex appeared to be counting the tiles of the coffered ceiling. Paco laughed under his breath.

"Where's the—" Madison stood as Paco pointed down the hall to the nearest bathroom, then rose with Ted and Rex while she rushed away from the table.

As she exited the room, Ted and Rex breathed out loud sighs of relief, and Paco placed reassuring hands firmly on their shoulders. "Well, gentlemen, I'm pretty sure the evening will only go downhill from here."

Ted and Rex nodded in vehement agreement before tidying up and scurrying out the door. They shouted their good-byes to Madison and left.

Paco took a moment to refresh his drink, then headed to the balcony to reel in a few emotions that were begging to break to the surface.

Madison's meek little steps approached. "Hello?"

"Out here," Paco called out, luring her to the balcony.

Her gasp of delighted approval gave him a strange sense of pride in his place. Approval wasn't in his vocabulary. He never sought it out. But somehow, it felt good, and he took in the sweeping city views differently, noticing every bright colorful twinkle across the skyline.

"God," she whispered, "and I thought this place couldn't get more amazing."

As a gust of crisp evening air hit them, Madison shivered a little. Paco took the opportunity to drape an oversize pashmina across her shoulders. She pulled it tight as she stood next to him on the balcony, looking out into the dazzling sparkles twinkling in the darkness.

"So, did everything come out all right?" Paco said, teasing her.

"Yes, and became a casualty of the three-second rule. So, I take it I scared the fellas off?"

"Hey, best poker game ever," he said, assuring her with a shoulder nudge. "If you want a cappuccino or nightcap, I could call Enrique to come up."

"Enrique?"

"Yes, my pool boy."

Madison beamed. "You have a pool?"

Pure mischief laced his words as he sang, "*Nooo*," and they both chuckled. "But he makes a great cappuccino, among other things."

Paco hung his head, turning somber. "Listen, sorry about grilling you earlier. I didn't mean to. I was just . . . disappointed in a certain someone." He looked over, catching her wince.

"I'm sorry, Paco."

"Sorry? *You* have nothing to be sorry about," he said, wrapping his arm around her shoulders, rubbing her tension away.

"I'm just, I don't know . . . not ready for what it means to bring the worldly Alex Drake to a wedding as my date."

Paco stood quietly. The best way to get information was always through silent, attentive listening. That, and he couldn't tip his hand that he'd assumed the opposite.

"Bringing Alex to a wedding when I'm the maid of honor is like bringing him home for Christmas dinner during a family reunion. There'll be a lot of attention. And questions. And what do I say? We're still getting to know each other, and there's so much still . . . unanswered."

Clasping his hands tightly together, Paco leaned on the railing, looking out and away. He could tell her. Answer all those unanswered questions. Give Madison the peace of mind she deserved.

But Alex asked her for a month, and she'd accepted. It was their agreement, not his. Like it or not, this was Alex's call. And whether he'd ever admit it to Alex's face, Paco respected the hell out of the man. So much so that he wouldn't interfere.

Despite being shoulder to shoulder, he could feel Madison's distance. She'd give in, but at the cost of pulling away.

"I'm making such a big deal out of this," she said, wringing her hands. "It's ridiculous. I'll just invite him."

Paco gave her a paternal look. "Not on my account. You're perfectly entitled to your feelings. Validated, even. You want the whole story first, to know what you're getting into, and that's fair. Besides, having a date for a wedding isn't a big deal. And if you're very nice, I might have another option for you."

That put the shine back in her eyes. "Really?"

"Yes. But I need to check a few things first. No matter what, you'll have a date for the wedding, and Alex will be fine with it."

Madison looped her arm through his, leaning her head on his shoulder. Comfortable with him. The way it should be.

"You're like an incredibly stylish guardian angel. Thank you." Madison smothered a yawn as she spoke. "I should get going."

"Why? I have a ridiculously fabulous guest suite. Stay. You know Alex will be working at least three more hours. I need to chat with him anyway about business, and I'll let him know. Check it out. It's the last room down the hall."

"You sure?"

"Have you ever known me to be unsure?" He eyed her with the confidence of a man who had never been wrong. Even to his detriment.

Her warm smile kept him in the moment, and her soft peck good night on his cheek tugged his heart hard enough that she'd own that piece of it forever.

∽

As Madison made her way to the guest suite, Paco caught the faint buzz of his cell. *Perfect timing.* He answered quickly, eager to chat.

"How's the game?" Alex asked, faking his way through wanting to hear about Madison.

Paco knew way too much about the situation with the two of them. Their month-long agreement was almost done, and this was the longest they'd been apart since entering said agreement. Without a doubt, it was eating Alex alive, torturing him from the inside out, though he'd never let on.

"Game's over. I offered Madison my guest suite tonight. Said you'd be preoccupied with work for several hours more, but I thought her staying here would be best, with this whole wedding thing. Madison didn't want to get into it, but I know it's killing you."

Alex let out a long sigh. "She's not ready to go public, and I don't blame her. She has no idea who she's in bed with. Literally. How can I expect her to trust me when I'm obviously hiding the past?"

Exhausted, Paco tossed out a loaded question and his best advice. "Why not just tell her?" Saying he had nothing to lose would be pointless. Paco would do it differently, but this was Alex's call. "Thirty days is almost up anyway, and this full-on delay of the inevitable is doing nothing more than adding a daily row of cinder blocks to the growing brick wall between you."

Alex took his time considering Paco's words, like he always did before coming to the exact same conclusion, no matter what the topic.

"You're right," he said, acquiescing as if he had a choice. But Paco's smug grin lasted for half a second, with his words barely making a dent in Alex's emotional shield. "It's better she stays there tonight."

Yup. He's getting a shoe up the ass.

"Fine," Paco said. "Well, in other news, I've got a plan B lined up for this whole wedding fiasco, but I'm giving you the courtesy of disapproving. Doesn't mean I'll listen, but you're free to share your feelings. If you have any."

"What can I say? You're my plan B kind of guy. I trust you implicitly."

"Good. I've got a great little number for Madison's pic."

"Pic?"

"Yup. For her dating profile. I'm thinking of leading with *Have a boyfriend but need a guy for the night.* I'll let you know how it goes."

"What kind of plan B is that?"

"Oh, now you care. What happened to 'I trust you. Implicitly.'"

"Fine," Alex said, letting Paco imagine the vein bulging from the middle of his forehead.

Evil scheming—check.

"Fine, what?" Paco asked, faking genuine surprise.

"Fine. I'll take your fucking afternoon-talk-show shrink advice. I'll figure out something tonight."

"*And?*" Paco said insistently.

"And I'll tell Madison everything. *Tomorrow.* I'll tell her tomorrow."

CHAPTER 14

ALEX

Alex hung up the phone and lay back in bed. Shirtless, he glided his hand mindlessly over the scars across his chest as he let his thoughts drift. Each flaw and welt in his skin had, over time, become him. The point at which his past and present always converged. A testament. A reminder.

There are no second chances.

Are there?

Memories flipped though his mind like photographs, each image making his heart pound harder, pulsing loudly in his ears. He shuddered and his eyes slammed shut.

Fuck. I can do this. I have to do this.

The soft chimes of his phone tugged Alex back to the here and now, announcing a FaceTime request from *her*. Wiping away the beads of sweat from his brow, he sucked in a breath and answered.

Madison's image filled the screen, with soft eyes and a warm smile that always managed to chase away the demons inside. She was here. He could relax.

"Hey, beautiful," he said, his normal, nothing-to-worry-about facade in place. "Did you win big?"

"Hardly. And the game ended abruptly when I made a cherry disappear deep into my cleavage."

"What kind of poker is that?"

"Texas Hold'em."

"Well, I'd love an encore performance of seeing how you hold 'em."

"I bet you would."

"Might the big winner be free for lunch tomorrow? I'm taking some time away from the office, and I'd love to take you to your favorite place, wherever that might be."

"Well, since I'm about as picky as a goat, how about you surprise me with something you love. Something that makes you feel like home."

You make me feel like home, Madison.

"Deal." He watched her take two subtle yawns, which always meant she was seconds from falling into a deep sleep. "See you tomorrow. Sleep well."

"You too." With that, Madison kissed two fingers and pressed them to the screen.

He let her hang up, lying there with nothing but an emptiness so strong, he had to stop himself from racing over there, busting through the door, and curling his body up against hers.

Alex had the night to figure things out. Not that he would sleep, with his most common bedfellow being insomnia. He continued pushing past the flashbacks from a decade gone, turning away from the play-by-play loop that normally plagued his mind. Fighting for control against his quickening pulse and the perspiration gathering on his face and neck, he got out of bed.

Rather than succumb to the undertow of dark recollections, Alex did what he always did. Pushed himself to exhaustion. In his penthouse gym, he flipped a switch. Hit with bright lights, he paused for a second to allow his eyes to adjust.

Moving past the other equipment, he opted for his fail-safe.

The Zero Runner. It was the one machine that would give him the benefit of a ten-mile run while preserving what was left of his knees. Kicking up from zero to a heart-pounding pace, he felt his tension ebb.

How the fuck will Madison not blame me when I blame myself? Or not hate me when I . . . I hate myself? Or . . .

Alex upped his pace, trying to run as far away from the past as possible, despite it being planted so firmly deep inside him.

Or leave? Is there a hope in hell she won't leave?

CHAPTER 15

MADISON

In the early hours of the midmorning workday, Madison escaped to catch a quick break. Stealing just enough time to sit alone in an isolated corner of the local artisan coffee house gave her a respite between analyzing charts and trend analyses. She had exactly twenty minutes to lose herself in a tall, dark roast cappuccino, catch up on a little reading, and relax a little before the next two hours of studying eye-crossing graphs.

"May I join you?" The annoying voice was recognizable, but completely unwelcome.

Madison glanced up from her seat at the intimate café table to see Frank Seaver looking down on her with a disgusting grin. Seaver was a senior vice president of Excelsior/Centurion, or E/C, the largest competitor of DGI.

He was known for being sharp as a whip, a mediocre dresser, and one of the biggest assholes of all time, often flaunting his expertise by mansplaining his way through every conversation with a woman.

Seaver constantly bandied his title about, using his status in the reckless and manipulative way common to bullies, the acts of a desperate man eager to secure his position as president of the company one day. One day very soon, if all his bragging were to come true.

Without knowing him well, or really at all, Madison *knew* his kind. Years in the service industry might not count for much on a résumé, but they gave her a solid foundation for instantly gauging *people*. The good, the bad, and the buttheads.

Over the years, Madison had fine-tuned her own sixth sense about people, and this guy was bad news. She'd only seen him once or twice at DGI, but between his slovenly appearance, the bits of food that always seemed to be stuck in his teeth, and the way he looked every woman up and down—present company included—absolutely made her skin crawl.

"I'm actually waiting for someone," Madison said firmly, hoping her assertive tone would cover the lie.

True to form, he ignored her, promptly plopping his pompous ass in the seat next to hers and scooted his chair uncomfortably close.

Oh my God. His breath.

"Oh, you're waiting for me," he said before snapping his fingers for the waitress.

Shocked, Madison stared. *How rude.*

The annoyed server ambled over to take his order. "You snapped?"

"Large black coffee in a to-go cup," he said without looking at her, instead leering so hard at Madison's body, she set a menu between them.

If he tries to move it, he's getting a fork in his hand.

"As I was saying, you're waiting for me."

The young woman returned with his coffee, and Seaver promptly retrieved an obnoxiously large old flask from his inside blazer pocket.

Taking one whiff as he poured the amber liquid into his cup, Madison felt her blood boil, driving a wave of heat straight to her cheeks.

This is the jack-hole who almost cost me the job at DGI. Nearly knocked me over, dumped most of his liquor-laced coffee on my blouse, and didn't bother looking me in the eye before bolting away. Well, maybe he's irritated the barista enough to ensure booze isn't his only add-on.

"And *why* would I be waiting for you?"

As much as Madison wanted to toss her own coffee right into his smug face, she knew Seaver's reputation. His pastimes included obsessing over the bottom line and initiating corporate wars against his enemies. If he was targeting her, it had to do with DGI. Like it or not, it would be worth her time to listen.

Holding back her repulsion at the food stains clinging to a shirt that hadn't been washed, oh, ever, Madison sat attentively.

"Let's just say I'm about to make you a very wealthy woman," he said, sliding his palm onto her knee.

Rather than jabbing a fork into his chubby, hairy hand, she gently lifted it to the table, keeping hold of it in the pretense of paying the man some attention. Choking back the bile rising in her throat, she asked, "And how exactly are you going to do that?"

Madison forced a smile that Seaver returned—chunks of food and all.

"Well, I understand you just might have the upper hand at DGI. Am I correct?"

Frank Seaver was many things . . . arrogant, opinionated, and smelly. But *wrong*? A jackass like him didn't climb the corporate ladder by accident. *He's up to something.*

She probed him for more. "I'm just an analyst, so I'm really not sure where you're going with this, but I'd"—*gulp*—"love to know more." She wasn't sure how long she could keep this up, but painted on a smile that she hoped gave him an assurance he could tell her anything.

"My dear, do you know what a proxy vote is?"

Madison's eyes widened as her mind began spinning. *The son of a bitch is angling for a hostile takeover. But why approach me?*

Contemplative, she covered her emotions. Her concerns. "Maybe," she said, looking up as if struggling to think. "It has something to do with a person giving their voting power to someone else. I think."

What's he up to?

His smile emerged, brimming with the charm of a crocodile. "Very good. And for the kind of proxy voting I'm after, I'd like to make you an offer. For your vote."

Wary, Madison took a moment to think. Her DGI retirement shares would be pretty much worthless with her junior status at the company, and couldn't come close to what a hostile takeover would require. And there was no way this guy was stalking his way through the corporate directory, one employee at a time, trying to get their votes.

Frustrated, she blew out a breath. *Can he just get to the point already? Maybe there's a way to speed this along.*

"I'm afraid you're wasting your time. I'm not nearly the stakeholder you think I am." Madison didn't have to fake her baffled expression. Genuinely dumbfounded, she studied him for a moment. The man didn't come close to living up to his reputation.

Their discussion now over, Madison waved for the barista, but ever the charmer, Seaver swatted her away. After digging through a very worn leather attaché that had probably once belonged to a Roosevelt, he pulled a piece of paper from it.

From where she sat, Madison could see it was a copy of a piece of paper that had been crumpled in spots, with large tears from one side to the other. Tape seemed to be holding it together like pieces of an aged treasure map. Overly dramatic for the circumstances, he slid it to Madison.

What the hell? In her hands was a copy of the contract Alex had given her—the one relinquishing all he owned if he ever lied to her. *But I threw it away.*

After her first night at Alex's penthouse, she'd torn it up and tossed it without a second thought. It should have been gone forever.

An unexpected breeze from the shop's door opening nearly snatched the paper from Madison's hand, and she gripped it harder. "Um, where did you get this?"

"Aw, naive little girl, a savvy businessman never reveals his secrets." He sneered, triumph lighting his beady eyes. "And from your reaction, I'm guessing you didn't realize you are the new majority shareholder of DGI."

The nudge was all she needed to pretend to be in the dark, diligently examining the document as if for the very first time.

"For argument's sake," she said, "let's imagine this is a legitimate contract. Which is crazy. As I read this, in order for this, well, insane transaction to occur, Alex Drake would need to somehow lie to me. He hasn't."

"Oh, but I assure you, he *has*."

The only thing keeping Madison from vomiting at Seaver's disgusting tone was that good organic free-trade java shouldn't be wasted.

Again, he reached into the battered attaché and pulled out another piece of paper. This time, it was an image of a photograph, printed on standard letter-size paper from what looked to be a home printer. Despite the fact the guy was low on magenta, the image was unmistakable.

Front and center of an obvious wedding photograph stood an exotic and strikingly beautiful woman, maybe the most beautiful Madison had ever seen. Dressed in white and with a tulle veil pulled back behind her head, she carried a lavish bouquet of pale roses. On both sides of her stood the men who had become staples in Madison's everyday life—Alex and Paco.

Seeing the image managed to rip Madison's heart from her chest for this asshole to dissect. What made it worse was that the picture was beautiful, filled with joy and happiness. So perfect, it could be a layout for a national bridal magazine.

By the looks of Alex and Paco, this snapshot had to be recent. The salt and pepper strands at Alex's temples—the ones she'd run her fingers through so many times—were as much in view as his wide smile and sparkling eyes.

Maybe it's older than it looks. Maybe not.

Forcing a sip of her coffee down her throat, Madison choked back her tears and took a deep breath before responding.

Without looking up, she kept her voice steady, despite her pounding pulse and her breaking heart. "He never said he wasn't married."

Disgusted, she said it. No matter what was happening between her and Alex, she was merely a pawn to Seaver. But this pawn was determined to protect DGI from a scumbag like him.

"Loyal to the end? A noble quality, though somewhat misplaced. Oh, I promise you, we're going to take all that pain and anger of yours and transform it into cold, hard cash. He'll pay. He'll hurt. I swear."

The man practically hissed the last words, oblivious to the fact that Madison wasn't conceding. *God, read the room.*

Confident, he pulled out another photo, placing it on top of the first one. Unlike the laser-printed wedding picture, this was a real no-kidding photo, yellowing and slightly torn at one corner.

Growing number by the second, she picked up the small picture and took a good, long look. The bastard had the nerve to be pleased with himself, propping his elbows on the table as he grinned smugly at her. Like a sadistic ringmaster, Seaver obviously reveled in wounding a creature before breaking its spirit. And this blow cut her to the core.

Madison let out the slightest gasp but remained as silent as possible, taking in the image through the blur of tears. *This has to be fake. Doctored. It can't be real.*

Impatient for the first time since sitting down, Seaver pointed at the image and began what had to be a well-rehearsed monologue. "That there's your brave brother, Jack. Valiant soldier.

Dedicated son. Remarkable brother. Taken too soon. And next to him, well, you probably recognize that man. Don't you, Madison?"

She said nothing, barely registering her recognition of Alex.

"Alex Drake didn't just hire you, my dear. He hired you to play you the same way he played Jack. Well, not exactly the same," Seaver said with a smirk.

Desperately, Madison scrutinized the photo, partially to pull back the tears that threatened, and partially to figure out how this could be possible.

Her brother was in uniform, his freshly minted lieutenant bars indicating this had to be months before his death. And the man next to him was a much younger but still unmistakable Alex Drake, who had one arm around Jack's shoulders. The arm of another person was also around Jack's shoulders, but from the other side. But the picture was cropped, and that person might never be known.

The furious look she shot at Seaver had no effect. In fact, he seemed pleased, smiling as he sipped his coffee. But her glare wasn't moving from him, and after a minute, he leaned in. In a full breath of coffee, cheap booze, and halitosis, he snarled his words.

"Your anger is misdirected. But you can take it out on Alex Drake—the man responsible for your brother's death."

In an instant, she dropped her gaze. There was no stopping the tears, so why bother trying?

Biting her lip, Madison struggled to make sense of it. Any of it. She and her father had both investigated Jack's death for years, but the government had closed ranks. Her family had learned nothing about the cause of Jack's death or the circumstances surrounding it. Not one thing.

Maybe a mogul like Alex Drake could shut down an investigation. But could he be a murderer? He obviously knew Jack—why not tell her so?

Every second she thought it through pushed more of a single emotion to the surface. The one she'd been fighting. The one nagging at her for weeks—doubt.

I don't know Alex at all.

With her last shreds of composure, she held it together enough to ask, "Can I keep these? Verify their authenticity?" Madison's voice was so low, she wasn't entirely sure Seaver heard her.

"Of course, my dear." With that, he stood. "Nothing is possible without you. Our relationship will thrive on openness and trust for many, many years to come."

She felt his hand stroke her hair, but was too engrossed in a tidal wave of feelings to slap it away.

Seaver huffed out a laugh. "I'll help you get the closure you need while making you rich beyond your dreams. Let it soak in. Call me when you're ready. I'll take it from there."

He left his pristine, high-gloss business card on the table before tossing out a crumpled ten-dollar bill, letting it land in a wad in her coffee cup. Finally, he swaggered out of the coffee house, his footsteps taking forever to disappear down the block.

Madison collected the photos and pieced-together contract and tucked them into her bag, then pulled out her wallet. Her hands shaking, she slipped out a twenty as the barista hurried over to stop her.

"He paid, hon. You're good."

I'm good? The last thing I am is good.

On the verge of uncontrollable bawling, Madison laid the twenty-dollar bill on the table. Wide-rimmed dark sunglasses would be her only defense against the tears now flowing freely.

"He's not buying my coffee. Or me."

CHAPTER 16

MADISON

In a daze, Madison wandered the city, eventually ending up where she'd started. A place she felt safe. The only place she could sink into the quicksand of emotions on the verge of engulfing her. And the only place that had nothing to do with Alex Drake. At all.

Exhausted, she found herself back home.

As soon as she walked through the door of her apartment, she collapsed under the weight of devastation. Her crying seesawed between light and controlled sobs to hysterically bawling. The worst came when she thought of Jack.

All her sorrow and pain poured out in the back-and-forth loop that replayed every detail of the days after her brother's death. The military notification. The return of his effects. The delivery of his remains. The funeral.

But the tragedy that didn't end with him. Jack was everything, and the shock waves of loss hit everyone, ripping her family apart.

After Jack's death, her father could barely function, and her mother couldn't bear living with a ghost of a man while dealing with her own loss of their son. The divorce happened so fast, tearing Madison from her father. Visitations were occasional, at best. Rebuilding that relationship took time. Madison hadn't just lost her brother—she'd also lost her father, and in many ways, she'd lost herself.

Barely fifteen at the time, she'd dealt with everything the way any teen would. Day by day, as best she could, not having much of a say or a choice. Her days were spent building a life around the hole in her heart, but never really filling it.

And today, that hole had been ripped open with cruelty and raw pain, shattering a very vulnerable side of her soul.

A long time passed before she had the strength to move from the spot she'd collapsed in. Little by little, she found enough strength to pick herself back up. Aimlessly, Madison scanned the untouched room.

Her apartment was exactly as she'd left it nearly a month ago. She'd moved into Alex's luxury penthouse before completely unpacking. Boxes were everywhere, stacked here and there, their contents waiting for her attention. She'd been too wrapped up in launching her career. And a new life. And her relationship with him. *Too goddamned wrapped up in Alex Drake.*

Well, not today. Today, right now, this moment was about Jack. And her family. About honoring the life of her brother and bringing all she had out into the light. Every photo. Every memento. Reclaiming the world she'd been robbed of. But...

What about the book?

Her book. From her grandfather. Another loss.

I have to get it back.

Across the small space, the microwave clock in the kitchenette gave her the time. A few hours lost, but the day could still be salvaged. Alex would still be at work. The penthouse would be empty.

I can run in and out, but then what? What happens after that?

Pushing back her uncertainty, she didn't know and didn't

care. Seeing the finish line wasn't important. This was a fresh start.

In haste, Madison grabbed her bag and flung open the door. About to bolt, she was stopped by the liar himself. Alex Drake stood there, staring down at her, holding his fist in mid-knock.

Seeing him now was too much.

It wasn't the anger and rage that consumed her. It was regret. Regret at gazing into those mesmerizing eyes and remembering the first time he'd knocked on a door that she'd opened. The first tender moments of something meaningful. Magical. Unlocking his world so completely, he'd captured her heart.

But now? Seeing the gorgeous man—the manipulator—was the last thing she needed.

CHAPTER 17

ALEX

"Madison, my God. We've been worried." Concerned, Alex studied her eyes. They were red and swollen and . . . unfamiliar. Wild. Dark. Maybe enraged. "What's wrong? What's happened?"

Opening his arms wide, Alex took a step toward her, ready to embrace her. But wide-eyed, she backed away. When his panic surged into overdrive, his instincts took over, shifting his approach from concerned boyfriend to trained operative.

Instantly, he dropped his arms and softened his demeanor. Focusing, he relied on the skills that always took over in a crisis, defusing the fragile situation he now found himself a part of. He took a step back to give her space as his mind spun with one too many worst-case scenarios.

What the hell is going on?

Alex took small, deliberate steps, crossing the threshold and entering, but left the door ajar, showing Madison she was free to leave or stay. That she was safe.

The lines in her brow deepened as she shifted her gaze from Alex to the door. Maybe her anxiety was stronger than he thought. It could be a panic attack. But it felt like fear.

She doesn't seem to know me. And she's afraid.

She had to open up. Forcing her out of this wasn't the answer. Whatever the hell this was, it would take patience. And time.

Alex steadied his voice, lowering it to a calm, commanding level. "Madison, please talk to me. You can tell me anything. What happened?"

Her expression was contorted. Conflicted.

With very slow movements, he motioned toward the sofa, silently asking if they could have a seat. When she gave him a begrudging nod, he made his way around a few boxes to the couch. Though there was plenty of room on the seat next to him, his gestured invitation was met with no response. No movement. No sound. Subtly, he offered the chair across from him, giving her any possibility to relax and sit.

Madison held out for a moment, pulling in a shuddering breath before lowering herself onto a chair across from him. Her glare was desperate. Exasperated. And by the look of those swollen, red-rimmed eyes, she'd been drained of every emotion and tear. Still, she clutched at her purse for dear life, creating a barrier between them.

Alex recognized the signs. *Shock. She's in shock. Coaxing her too quickly might backfire.*

"Take all the time you need," he said calmly, almost hypnotically, before lowering his elbows to his knees, leaning forward and trying like hell to gain any shred of insight.

Madison's clothes were intact. No sign of struggle. No contusions. No marks. Nothing from an impact. Nothing physically traumatic to give him a clue at what could have happened to her. Nothing other than her big, beautiful eyes, ravaged by tears.

Contemplative, Madison studied Alex without a word until finally, her gaze lowered. After what seemed like an eternity, she cleared her throat, beginning with a question.

"How did you know where I was?"

Pointing to the purse she clutched like a teddy bear, he gave her a soft, matter-of-fact response. "Your corporate phone has a tracker. We had a lunch date. I thought you might have been tied up, but when I heard you'd missed several meetings and hadn't used your keycard to reenter the building, I panicked. Madison, please, can you tell me what's going on?"

After another small eternity of silence where Alex could do nothing but be patient and sit still, Madison finally spoke. "Tell me something, Mr. Drake. Are you married?" she asked, and the sight of her trembling lower lip killed him. She was heartbroken, and he had no idea why.

Surprised, he sat up straighter. "No, I'm not. Why would you think that?"

Glaring at him, Madison dug into her purse and whipped out what seemed to be Exhibit A. "Looks like the happy couple and his best friend."

Alex took the photo. Tamping down his alarm, he raked his fingers through his hair, controlling the tremble as his hand worked the tense area of his neck.

"That's exactly what it is," he muttered under his breath, staring hard at the image.

The matter-of-fact tone of his admission was probably the worst thing he could do with Madison, but he couldn't do more. *It can't be. Not again.*

Abruptly, Alex stood. Raising his voice startled her, but this was as controlled as he could be at the moment. "Madison, where did you get this?" He thrust it at her, snapping the sheet abruptly.

Pissed off and defiant, she snatched it back. "Is that all you can say? You're married, shacking up with me like I'm a kept woman, and all you can ask is where I got this? Who the hell do you think you are?"

Blankly, Alex stared. "Madison, there's a lot going on here, but please believe she's not my wife. I can expl—"

"Then whose wife is she? God, with all the secrets and bullshit, you'd think I'd be okay with this. News flash. I'm not."

Madison's voice was cool and cutting, but its venom made

something completely clear. She might have been his at one point, but she wasn't his now.

The click of the door shutting gave Madison a jolt, and she spun toward it as the printout she held slipped from her fingers and landed at Paco's feet. Worry dulled his usually cheerful demeanor as he glanced at Alex, who had nothing for him but an apologetic look.

After locking the door, Paco scooped up the picture, his expression hardening as he stepped closer to Madison. "Yasmin isn't Alex's wife. She's mine."

CHAPTER 18

ALEX

Alex watched as Madison reeled from her raw emotions. "*Yours?*"
Before Paco could respond, Alex cut in.
"Madison, it's a long story, too long to explain now, but this is very, very important. Where did you get this?" When he tried stroking her arm, she whipped it away, so he did the only thing he could think of. He begged. "Please."
Not wasting time, Paco pulled out a small old-school flip phone. With an authority that seemed natural to him, he said three words. "Omega is compromised." Then he hung up.
The gravity of the situation was suffocating. There was no way for Madison to know. To comprehend.
Timidly, she said, "The man who gave me that also gave me this." Pulling the small photo from her purse, Madison reluctantly held it up to Alex.
Paco moved closer, eyeing it too. The glance he and Alex exchanged was solemn.
And then she said it, words Alex could never unhear. A question that came from the only woman he'd let in, see him unshielded, know how damaged he was. It shattered any hope of a future for them. There was no turning back.

"Alex, did you—" She choked back her tears. "Did you have something to do with my brother's death?"

Stunned, Alex stood there in disbelief. Paco stepped in, ever protective of his best friend, even with Madison. But the trembling hand Alex lifted stopped Paco cold.

It was Alex's turn to step back, to look at this woman like a stranger, and defend himself to the only person who had the power to be both his judge and jury. With a deep breath, he barely uttered the word, "No."

It was then that Alex realized the truth. Despite opening his world to Madison—his life—she didn't know him at all. Maybe, somehow, that was unfair. If he took a step back and looked at this objectively, maybe her perspective was understandable. But still, the accusation hit him like the blast wave of a nuclear bomb.

Since they first met a couple of months ago, he'd wrestled with how to tell her the whole story. The tragedy he and Madison shared. The senseless chain of events that bound them, bringing them all through a world of anguish to arrive at this very point. Yes, unpacking years of pain was inevitable. But he'd never imagined she'd assume he was remotely involved in Jack's death. Or worse, responsible.

Devastated and settling into his own fresh hell of shock, Alex switched back to autopilot—his last bastion of self-defense. Slipping back into a way of life he'd thought was over, dealing with the crisis of the moment, while suffocating everything else until it was lifeless and numb.

For people like Alex, life was a string of old habits that keep one day rolling into the next. He knew what he needed to do. What the situation demanded of him. And right now, he needed to leave.

Emotionless, he moved to the door. "Paco, stay with Madison. I'll take care of Yasmin."

But just as he stepped outside the apartment, Paco caught up and his strong grip wrapped around Alex's arm, holding him in place.

"What do you mean? Madison needs you." Paco leaned closer, lowering his voice. "And you need her."

The slight tremble that started quickly grew until it rocked through Alex, steadily overtaking his body in a full quake. In one sharp move, he broke free, his open palm landing on Paco's chest. "We don't have time for this. Omega requires cleanup. Epsilon is being activated."

Controlled, Paco held his wrist, huffing out his annoyance. Even though Alex had forty pounds on his friend, he was no match for a pissed-off Paco, and they both knew it.

"Goddammit, Paco!"

Instantly, Paco's expression morphed from faithful friend to *go fuck yourself*. Releasing Alex, he scowled as he crossed his arms across his chest.

"I'm sorry," Alex said, knowing he'd gone too far. If anyone had suffered, it was Paco. He had every right to demand to take point for protecting Yasmin.

Looking away, Alex shoved his hands in his pockets, a feeble attempt to mask how bad the tremors were getting. His voice calmed. "Look at Madison. She can't even make eye contact, let alone have me anywhere near her. I'm no good here. I'm—" Alex cleared his throat and clenched his teeth, trying hard to conceal the flush he could feel rising up his cheeks, and the heat saturating his ears.

Relenting, Paco unfolded his arms. After all their years together, he obviously knew what Alex needed now. Space. The quiet and isolation of a drive would let him breathe. Snap him out of it quicker.

"Okay," Paco said, clapping his back.

"I'll take care of Yasmin, I swear." Alex's words were factual but pleading, and he laid a reassuring hand on Paco's shoulder. "Nothing will happen to her. This isn't a full compromise. We don't know how much has been exposed. It's just . . . a precaution."

"I know," Paco said, perhaps trying to convince both of them.

Businesslike and focused, Alex retrieved his phone. "And you—you take care of Madison. Find out what happened. And . . ."

He glanced through the doorway. Despondent, Madison paced in her living room, wiping fresh tears from each cheek.

"Tell her—tell her everything." With a glance that exchanged their understanding, Alex rushed out, hurriedly pressing his phone to his ear.

CHAPTER 19

MADISON

Madison looked up to find Paco entering. Alone. Her shoulders drooping with a combination of relief and disappointment, she tried to control her shaking body and hold back her tears as she spoke.

"Paco, I don't know what's going on, but if I've done something that put someone in danger—"

In a few long strides, he wrapped his arms around her, rocking her with a tight hug. Her trembling subsided in his hold.

"Hey, you haven't," he said softly, which only made her sob harder. "Shhh. Yasmin will be fine. Alex will take care of it. He always does."

"He will?" It felt traitorous to say it again. To doubt Alex. Openly. But she had to hear Paco's response. To know.

He pulled away enough to look her in the eye, his expression unyielding. "Yes, he will. Look, Madison, it's really important that we know who's been pushing all this to you. It's a dirty little trick we call playback. They're feeding you misinformation in a way that looks real, but it's all smoke and mirrors to manipulate you. Gain intel." He cupped her cheek and forced her sad eyes to meet his. "We don't have a lot of time. We need to know who's after Yasmin."

Madison broke their embrace to grab her handbag and retrieve the battered contract, which she passed to Paco.

"As far as I know, they're not after your, um, wife," she said, and when he smiled at her hesitation, she told him the rest. "I think they're after Alex."

"Who are?" Paco asked as his phone buzzed. He took a moment to check. "It's Alex," he said, answering and turning on the speakerphone. "I have you on speaker. Madison shed some light on the situation. I'm not sure we're blown. Maybe just inadvertently exposed."

"Then what's this about?" Alex asked, his voice sounding steady and calm.

"Apparently, it's personal." Paco urged Madison with his eyes.

"Alex," she said, struggling to speak. "I th—think they're after you."

"Is that all?" he asked in that casual tone she'd gotten to know. It was easygoing. Reassuring. His way of protecting her. "This isn't my first rodeo. But I usually tend to keep my enemies closer. Who's targeting me?"

Disappointed to admit it, Madison said, "Frank Seaver."

"There's more," Paco said. "He had the contract you gave Madison."

Blubbering, Madison wanted to clarify. To explain. But she had no explanation. "I swear, I have no idea how he got it."

"Shhh." Paco rubbed her back gently, soothing her. "Alex, you still there?"

"Yes. Still here. I might be pushing a hundred miles an hour away from you two, but I'm not going anywhere."

His words lifted her heart in a way she couldn't understand. But this was Alex. The guy who'd said those same words when she fell apart after the parachute jump. As if he'd say it over and over again for the rest of their lives if he had to.

"Look," Alex said. "Epsilon is in motion. It's a good idea to maintain course. I'll wrap that up, which will probably take another two hours. If you don't hear from me, we'll circle back at the penthouse. But can you give me a moment with Madison?"

As requested, Paco toggled off the speakerphone, then handed the phone to her and stepped away. Her gaze followed him for a minute in the small space as he seemed to be deciding if he should step outside. Instead, he seemed to find the perfect excuse to slip inside her bedroom.

"Madison?"

"Yes, I'm here. Alex, I'm—"

"Don't say a word. Just listen. I know you're confused and unsure, and that's my fault. All of this could have been avoided if I'd just told you everything up front. But, as you're probably figuring out, it's complicated. I'm complicated."

"No, you're—" She paused, afraid to finish. *The only thing I need right now.*

"I'm ready to uncomplicate things. Seaver's gunning for a hostile takeover bid. They'll end up offering me a golden parachute, a huge lump-sum buyout to ensure I walk away quietly. Considering my options, maybe walking away isn't the end. Maybe, beautiful, it's a beginning. For us."

"What?" Madison asked softly. "Alex, what are you saying?"

A golden parachute? That's insane. A pile of money that would push him out of Drake Global Industries forever?

"You can't step down from DGI. You *are* DGI."

From memory, Madison could recite every major corporate milestone. List every office throughout the world. Every award. Alex Drake had built a garage startup into a billion-dollar empire. His fingerprints were on every achievement and honor. Without Alex Drake, there was no Drake Global Industries.

I can't let this happen.

"Truth is," he said, "I've been fighting for a lot of years now. I don't want to fight anymore. I want to wake up and know that I haven't wasted another day on meaningless work. To know that at the end of the day, I've got something wonderful to look forward to." He paused a moment. "And I know it's unfair to say it, but I don't care about any of it. I just want you, Madison."

She couldn't think of what to say or do, but this was one grand gesture she couldn't accept. "Alex—"

"Paco can tell you anything you want to know. Everything. And tomorrow, I've cleared my calendar. If you want to talk, or meet, or anything at all . . ."

She could hear the interruption of an incoming call. Someone else was demanding his attention, and she knew it was important.

"Madison, I'm sorry, but I need to take this. Just know that I'm here for you. I'll always be here for you."

With that, the call ended, and the phone clicked back to the home screen. Alex was gone.

Staring hard and wishing him back was no use. A whimpering sigh escaped her. So much had been left unsaid.

When Paco emerged from her bedroom, wearing one of her oversize T-shirts, pajama pants, and fuzzy pink slippers, Madison's instant smile was unavoidable. It was obvious the man could never be trusted with her stuff. The pale pink T-shirt had a queen logo across the front, making it doubly apropos.

He hopped on her couch, crisscross-applesauce style, and encouraged her to do the same. When she did, he took both her hands in a firm grip. He held them to his chest, meeting her eyes with a tender expression.

"There's a lot for us to talk about. I'd rather be comfortable if I'm going to bare my soul tonight. How about you put on some pajamas while I rustle up snacks and drinks?"

With a relieved inhale, Madison nodded in agreement, but snacks might be a problem since she hadn't lived there in weeks. Plus, a stocked refrigerator? Uh, serious backburner stuff there.

"I don't think I have any groceries. And any I do have are

probably a science experiment just begging for a YouTube channel."

The doorbell rang, and Paco jumped to his feet to answer as Madison followed. The delivery man outside was loaded down with an assortment of deliciously fragrant Chinese food, and a large brown paper bag filled with a bottle of Grey Goose vodka and all the fixings for Paco's sexed-up cosmos, including the ice and glasses. *Because the man is an absolute genie.*

"We're all set." After a quick inventory, Paco motioned the delivery man to the small table, where he carefully set the bags.

As Madison rummaged through them, he yanked her by the hips, shooing her away.

"Change first. Comfy jammies and comfort food to get us through this night." Under his breath, his voice was strained. "We're gonna need it."

It was clear Paco was trying to dress up a pile of crap with her favorite foods and some warm comfort. As he worked to set everything up in the cramped space, she gave him a hug from behind before dutifully obeying and reacquainting herself with her comfiest loungewear.

With the bedroom door cracked open, she could hear Paco clanking about and fixing their drinks. In his best Bette Davis impression, he drawled, "Fasten your seat belts. It's going to be a bumpy night."

The man was freaking adorable. She could hear him give the cocktail shaker a fierce rattle before pouring. Peeking out, she caught him downing one, pursing his lips with disapproval at the empty glass before drinking the other. Apparently, their impending discussion had a two-drink minimum.

"Hey, save some for me," she called out.

"Don't worry. There's plenty where that came from." Soon, there was another rattle of the shaker as he promptly fixed another round.

Paco looked up as Madison returned. She wasn't exactly the

girl next door. More like the girl next door's comfy cousin. Her wavy locks were wound into a bun on top of her head, and her pink fleece robe was tightly cinched, revealing only the bottoms of her flannel pajama pants and fuzzy panda slippers.

Hands on her hips, she admired the slight wobble to his stance. "And exactly how many am I trailing by?"

"Three," Paco said with a strong roll of his *r*. Curiosity washed over his expression. "What's under the robe?"

"Oh, just a shirt."

"Come on . . . let's see your go-to undisputed number one comfy shirt of all time."

With a roll of her eyes, Madison loosened her robe, tugging it open to reveal a very worn and extra-snug e.t. the extra-terrestrial T-shirt. When Paco's eyebrows rose with amused judgment, Madison sternly cautioned him. "Not a word."

On cue, one eyebrow dropped. The judgy one. The amused one held its ground, prompting her to explain.

"Jack gave it to me for my eighth birthday. It's my favorite movie of all time, and wearing it somehow always makes me, I don't know, feel better. Like everything's going to be all right. And before you go thinking *E.T.* is juvenile, Neil Diamond wrote the song 'Heartlight' because it's such a beautiful movie."

Paco seemed to be feeling every ounce of the effects of that third cocktail. Genuinely fascinated, he asked, "Really?"

CHAPTER 20

MADISON

With cocktails poured, Chinese food in hand, and "Heartlight" softly playing from Paco's phone, Madison and Paco both tended to their boxes of chow mein, each equally adept at using chopsticks. Paco ate quietly, quelling any conversation for most of the meal. Even his chewing was unnervingly soft.

Done picking at her food, Madison set the takeout box on a side table. Staring at Paco, she wondered how long he intended to stall with this girls-night-in setup. Or how bad the blow was to come.

Paco finished off a last mouthful of noodles and stood. Gathering the remnants of their meals, he tossed them in the garbage can in the kitchen, then grabbed the tall bottle of liquid courage on his way back.

He took a breath, stopped the music on his phone, and returned to his place on the couch.

Beseeching him with hopeful eyes and a wry smile, she wasn't sure what to ask or how to start, but thankfully didn't need to decide. After a swig straight from the vodka bottle, Paco wedged it between his lotus-crossed legs, then started with a question of his own.

"Madison, what do you know about Jack's death?"

After a few seconds, she forced out an honest response. "Nothing at all, I guess. The military wouldn't say a word about what happened or even where he was or what he'd been doing."

Thoughtfully, Paco sipped from the bottle again. "Where's that picture you had?"

Madison took it from the end table and carefully handed it to him. Taking a moment to look it over, he smiled slightly before he turned it toward her. Holding it up to give her another look, he let it dangle from his fingertips with his knuckles facing her.

"What do you see?" he asked.

Her gaze followed the figures in the photo, first examining Jack and then Alex. Uncertain, she looked back at Paco, shaking her head slightly.

Shrugging, she said, "I see Jack and Alex. It had to be right after Jack's commission as an officer. And Alex is much younger than now, maybe about the same age as Jack. It had to be just . . . before."

She didn't elaborate on *before what*. It was clear Paco understood.

Insistent, he held the photo higher. "Look again, Madison."

He wasn't angry. If anything, his tone was softer. Sincere.

Madison did as he asked, determined to find whatever she had to be missing.

Following the line of the mystery man's hand, her eyes caught the smallest clue, and she leaned closer. Gasping, she made the discovery. The one Paco nodded to as she searched his eyes for confirmation.

As Paco held the photo for her, his expression melted, and she reached out to traced the ring on his finger. His pinky ring. It was the same one on the hand of the man just out of the photo. The man was Paco.

"You were there?" Madison asked, watching the exaggerated nods of a man pickled and boozed.

"I was there," he said somberly. "I was there when it happened. All of it. Every—" He choked up, pinching the bridge of his nose hard, not quite stopping his own tears from forming.

"Why are you cut out of the photo?" Madison wondered aloud, her finger tracing that side of the photo and noticing for the first time that the edge was frayed. It was subtle, but up close looked as though the paper had been creased repeatedly, then torn.

With a huff, he took another swig. "I'll get to that. But I need to start with the night it happened. The night Jack . . ."

Snapping his eyes shut, Paco took a moment, and Madison laid a hand on his knee. Regaining his composure, he started again, now running his thumb over Jack's smiling image.

"Jack and I were recruited separately. They were seeking military members who possessed . . . special skills, you could say. Well, except Alex."

"Alex?" Madison traced a finger over his image. "Why isn't he wearing a uniform?"

"Because Alex wasn't military. He wasn't one of us." Paco pulled the photo closer and blinked to regain his focus. "God, I hated that son of a bitch back then."

His rough words were oddly endearing. Paco took more than a swig before continuing. It was enough of a gulp to push him past his discomfort and continue.

"So, there we were, the three of us in a Jeep, in the pitch black of night, right in the heart of BFE, when Alex's Spidey sense kicks in. The man could feel things. Anxious, he insisted on taking a look around. That didn't go over well with Jack, who told him to keep his ass in the Jeep."

"That sounds like Jack," Madison said, remembering him fondly.

"At which point Alex hopped out."

"Which sounds like Alex."

"Yup. Alex didn't care. None of us answered to each other.

And Jack and I . . ." Paco trailed off, looking at Madison as he chose his words. "Jack and I always had each other's back, and loyalty was a big deal with him. Just like with you."

With the tip of his finger, he lifted her chin as he motioned to the windowsill. A handful of pennies were neatly stacked in rows. It was a family pact she thought nobody knew about.

"I knew the consequences of not backing Jack. But I couldn't shake it. I grew up in the streets. Fighting is in my blood. Like Alex, I could feel something headed our way." Paco's expression was soft and apologetic before he dropped his gaze. "I wanted Jack to be right."

After a heavy breath, he pushed out the rest. "Alex and I both left the Jeep, tracking in opposite directions away from Jack's position. That's when it happened. Alex noticed something. Something neither Jack nor I did."

"What?"

Paco looked away, as if seeing the tragedy projected on a screen before him. "Signaling. Small white lights in the distance. They knew where we were. Alex raced toward the Jeep, screaming for Jack to get out. I ran back too, but we were both too late. The RPG hit. I could see him. Jack tried getting out, but couldn't clear the blast. The force of the explosion threw him, pelleting him with shrapnel as it threw his body far from me. Alex was closer, catching the white hot bumper right in the chest. It burned clear through his clothes, branding his skin. I was the luckiest, or the most damned of them all."

It took another swig for him to keep going.

"I got hit in the head with something." Pulling his hair back, he revealed a scar along his hairline. "But never knew what. It knocked me out cold. It was Yasmin who discovered me, a local girl. She and I both thought Jack and Alex were dead, so she led me to a cave in a small hill, hiding me there with no other plan beyond that. She brought me a little food and water, probably her own meal for that day. And within twenty hours, a cleanup crew arrived. They picked up my tracker. That's when I learned Jack and Alex had been medevac'd to Germany. They were both alive. At least, for the moment."

Madison scooted closer to Paco, weaving her fingers through his and resting her cheek on his shoulder. His head, heavy from the booze, fell willingly on hers. He squeezed her hand, rubbing light circles along her thumb.

"By the time I got to Germany, Jack was barely holding on. Alex, though stable, was unconscious most of the time, thanks to morphine. He only woke for moments here and there, but just enough to see me give Jack one last good-bye." He took another gulp from the bottle.

Madison pulled away enough to look at Paco, watching fresh trails of tears stream down his cheeks before dropping into his lap.

"I kissed Jack. One last time before he passed."

It took a second to take that one in. Madison had never considered that her brother might be gay, but hadn't really thought about his sexuality at all.

It did explain why despite invitation after invitation to homecomings and proms, Jack never went. And it gave her even more insight into the pieces of a puzzle that had never quite clicked together. Her mind flipped through dates and places. Overheard conversations. Letters.

Yes, the letter. Perhaps she had a revelation of her own to share.

Cupping Paco's face, Madison gently swept her thumbs across his tears. For a passing second, she left a tender kiss on his cheek, then hugged him tightly. "It was you."

Paco pulled back. "What was me?"

"Jack mentioned you." She took both of his hands and squeezed. "He told us about you. Wanted to introduce you to us when he got back. But we didn't know who you were. Not even your name." She squeezed a little tighter. "All he said was that you were, and I quote, the love of his life."

Paco lowered his forehead to hers, and they sat there a moment, soaking it all in.

"I have to tell you the rest," he said with a shiver, and Madison grabbed the nearby throw and wrapped it around his shoulders.

"Alex had a much longer recovery, and they were about to send me back to the States. But I visited Alex, wanting to see him before I left, and gave him the book. That way, he'd have something to pass the time. And to remember Jack by."

Madison was puzzled. "A book?"

Paco just looked back, giving her a *keep up* expression. "No, not a book. *The* book. You know."

"Oh my God." Hopping to her feet, she headed to her bedroom. There, on the dresser, was the book in question. *The Count of Monte Cristo,* exactly where she'd left it.

She grabbed it and returned to Paco, who was now sprawled across the length of the couch with the blanket pulled up to his chin. Squinting open one eye, he lifted his feet, letting her sit down before resting his legs across her lap.

Pausing to pull in a deep breath and release it, Madison opened the cover, and there it was. The identical inscription that their grandfather had penned in both her copy of the book . . . and Jack's.

Love you always. Grandpa Mike.

This was it. The answer. The first time she'd doubted Alex was about the copy of this book with the same inscription that she'd found in his penthouse. Believing it was hers, she'd demanded to know where he'd gotten it from and didn't believe his story, but everything he'd said was true. It was given to him. And it wasn't her book after all.

Repeatedly, she shook her head in amazement. "Of course.

Jack had a copy too. I guess I should have known. Grandpa Mike always made sure we had the same gifts. Mostly to keep me from having a freak-out, because I always had to have exactly what Jack had." Her fingers walked across the inscription. "But why didn't Alex just tell me?"

Paco chuckled. "Oh, that." He stacked his hands behind his head, laughing at the memory. "That would be because your older brother insisted."

Wide-eyed, Madison considered his statement, convinced that the thought of Jack having any say in her future dating had to be the ramblings of a thoroughly intoxicated man. She was a teen when Jack died, so for him to make any demands of Alex regarding her was ridiculous. Her skeptical expression pressed Paco to explain.

"One night, we were all playing five-card stud, and just, you know, shooting the breeze. As usual, Jack starts going on with his Frankie stories. Frankie this. Frankie that. Which, by the way, were so freaking adorable."

Madison couldn't help but smile at the memory of the nickname her brother had given her when they were kids.

"Alex, being the cocky bastard he was, popped off that when you grew up, he was going to marry you. He said it just to piss Jack off, and it worked. The thought of Alex being Jack's brother-in-law was enough to make him double-down."

"Sounds about right."

"But Jack gave you a lot of credit. Said a slick-talking womanizing bastard like him didn't stand a chance with his Frankie."

Awkward.

"And that's when Alex had to go into some story about the Italian twins, and—" Paco quickly cut himself off, obviously feeling the weight of Madison's glare. "But that's not the point," he said, recovering quickly. "The point is that Jack threw Alex a challenge. If by some twist of fate Alex ever met you—once you were of legal age, of course—"

"Of course."

"Jack was sure Alex wouldn't last thirty days with you, and that you'd never want to be with such a money-hungry, skirt-chasing son of a bitch. Oh—" Despite the Botox, Paco's brow furled.

With his hand smacked hard to his lips, he apologized. "Sorry. That's sort of a direct quote. And for whatever ass-backward reason, Alex took it literally. Maybe because those were some of the last words Jack ever said to him. Like he'd made a commitment."

"Because that's Alex Drake. A man who keeps his commitments," Madison said before giving Paco a curious look. "But that doesn't explain the photo."

"Oh, why I'm torn out of it? I was visiting Alex, giving him the book. Even in his condition, in pain and being pumped full of every legal opiate known to man, he was sharp. He overheard a conversation. A cover-up was about to go down, and Jack was chosen to be the fall guy for an operation gone very, very wrong. Seriously, those idiots thought dead men wouldn't talk. Well, I sure as hell wasn't dead."

"Who?" Madison asked, not sure she wanted that answer.

Paco only shrugged. "I don't know, and back then, I didn't care. But if I was going to take on this battle, I had to protect everyone else from the backlash. If those bureaucratic assholes would pin this on a dead veteran, nothing was sacred, and a smear campaign would be way too easy for them. And I didn't know you—or your family. I had no idea what you'd think of me and Jack. So I figured I'd take on the fight alone. No collateral damage. I tore myself out of the photo but left the Jack-and-Alex half in the book. I knew Alex would like some memory of Jack. And I burned my side of it."

He thought for a minute, then wiped his eyes again. "You know, the saddest part is, it was the only photo of us together. Anyway, I made it to the Pentagon, and managed to get in front of all the key players. Threatened them with everything I had, which between us girls, wasn't fucking much. But I swore I'd talk. Welp, the sons of bitches kept their word, all right. They doctored Jack's official record to say that he separated from the service months before the operation. That meant no life insurance payout to his family. No combat casualty payment. Any benefits he would have left you and your family evaporated into thin air. Nothing but his name. Jackson Daniel Taylor."

It was insane. But Paco had to be so alone in all of this.

Patting his feet resting in her lap, Madison said, "I can't believe everything you did. I wish I could have been there for you . . . *we* could have been there for you."

Paco shook his head. "All Jack talked about was his family. About you." He sat up a little and reached out to caress her face. "I knew you'd need closure. You'd need to know Jack died with honor, even if you didn't know all the details. So, the veteran's funeral was arranged. I scraped together whatever money I could to make sure he had a beautiful service."

Perplexed, Madison stared at him. "Wait, I thought the military paid for his service."

"If the record said he died on active duty, they would have. Close to one hundred percent. But they screwed him, so he got a veteran's service instead. Still beautiful, but the benefits only covered transportation from Germany to Dover, and I still needed to get him home. Plus, the casket needed to be paid for, and several other things. I knew Jack had been sending money home, so it wasn't like you were swimming in dough."

Paco slumped back. "I didn't want to intrude on your family's privacy, so I did what I do best." He clumsily sipped again, spilling a little on his cheek, which Madison wiped up with her sleeve. "I became invisible. I worked behind the scenes with the funeral director, making sure that whatever your family needed was covered. Money was never discussed. I pawned the few gold chains I had, and some other things I could live without. At one point, I almost thought I'd have to give this up." He wiggled his pinky, highlighting the ring. "But it's just some cheap pot metal. Jack found it somewhere in Italy. Worthless to pawnshops, but priceless to me."

He planted a big kiss on the ring, then slipped it off just enough to give Madison a glimpse of the skin beneath. "See?"

Giggling, she gently caressed the green-tinged skin with her fingertips.

Beaming at her, his eyes glistened with tears. "You were so young. When I saw you, it reminded me of what Jack would have looked like at your age. Well, probably with shorter hair," he teased, wrapping a loose tendril of her hair around his finger, and sinking deeper into his comfy spot.

"After you and your family left, all I could think about was Yasmin. She was barely older than you. So young, yet so brave. She risked her life saving me. It was too late for Jack, but maybe not for Yasmin. I needed to do something. And that's when Alex Drake blew back into my life, and together . . ." Dramatically, he counted off with his fingers. "We found the girl. Rescued the girl. *I* married the girl. We thwarted one—no, two kidnapping attempts on Yasmin, and built a multibillion-dollar empire, *and* . . ." Paco looked around. "Uh, where's your bathroom?"

Quickly, Madison pointed to the bedroom, where the only bathroom was. "Through there. Do you need help?"

Fumbling his way toward the bedroom, Paco doubled over in laughter. "No, girlie. As helpful as you are, I've got this."

As soberly as possible, he disappeared into the bedroom, then instantly popped his head back out, leaning hard against the frame of the door.

"You know, about a year ago, Alex became obsessed with finding you. Really obsessed. Well, not obsessed with *finding* you, so much as wondering if you might miraculously pop into his life. Somehow. I guess finding you would've been too fucking easy for a guy with a global reconnaissance business."

"Seems to be a man who likes a challenge."

"But every time a woman crossed his path with the last name Taylor, he had me check into her. See if it was you. Jack never mentioned your name, just your nickname, Frankie. And I . . . I never told him I knew you. I mean, knew where you were."

Curious, Madison asked, "Why not?"

Fighting gravity, Paco slid down the door frame a little, then managed to pull himself back up again. "Because after Jack died, Alex nearly died too. Not just physically. It took a lot to get him out of the dark. For a time, nobody could even mention Jack without Alex lashing out or breaking down."

That makes two of us.

"Somehow, he felt responsible. Like if he'd just done things differently. Or reacted faster. I guess I wasn't quite sure he'd be good for anyone, least of all you."

With an accusatory finger pointed at her, Paco stood taller. "And *someone* helped him get him out of that dark, dark place, missy." A smile lifted his lips. "And it's someone *you* know," he taunted before disappearing into the bedroom again.

Madison heard several thuds, with items being knocked about. Obviously, Paco was finally making his way to the bathroom, one knocked-over item at a time.

The suspense was too much. "Wait," she called out. "Who do I know that helped Alex?"

Paco shouted back. "Dan."

Dan? "Dan who?"

"You know. Dan." A second later, he called out, "Taylor."

With that, Madison heard the bathroom door snap closed.

Dad?

CHAPTER 21

MADISON

Counting down the minutes, Madison impatiently awaited Paco's return.
Seriously, how long does it take to pee?
Flush? *Check.* Wash hands while faintly humming "Happy Birthday"? *Check and check.*
Finally, she could hear the bathroom door opening, but Paco didn't emerge. Another sixty seconds ticked by before she went to check on him.
There, having discovered a bed that was just right, Paco had pushed the covers to the side and passed out, one clear-coat-pedicured foot dangling over the other.
Tiptoeing to him, Madison laughed at the slightest little vodka-induced snore. About to bring the covers over him, she paused, again noticing his ring.
I guess that makes you my brother-in-law.
With a faux-down comforter, she tucked him in and kissed him gingerly on the temple. His suit jacket and pants were laid out on the other side of her full-size bed, delivering a rare once-in-a-blue-moon opportunity.
Making her way to the nightstand, she silently slid open the

drawer, pulling out an aged envelope as quietly as possible. With a few items of cheap jewelry, pens, an old pack of gum, and some cosmetic samples piled on top of it, she wasn't quiet at all. But Sleeping Beauty snored on, blissfully undisturbed.

The stamp on the envelope was beautiful, designed with flowers and a single word. *Italia.* It was the last note from Jack, mailed to her over a decade ago. After pressing her lips to it, Madison slipped the envelope into the pocket of Paco's custom blazer, ensuring it peeked out, but knocked over his slacks in the process.

Delighted, she recognized the key fob that fell onto the floor. Embracing the temptation of the heavy little device, she pushed aside the technical term for what she had in mind. *Grand theft auto.*

"I swear I'm just borrowing it," she whispered. Returning to the living room, she grabbed her bag and headed out, admiring the bright yellow Lamborghini parked at the curb.

He's seriously a little too trusting of this neighborhood.

After the driving lesson Paco had recently given her, she had the mechanics down, taking off with the rumble of the car drilling straight into her crotch. It was then that she bothered glancing down. There she was, in what could possibly be a half-million-dollar car, classing it up in her comfiest PJs, fuzzy robe, and smiling panda slippers.

For a hot second, turning around crossed her mind, but she rejected the thought.

It's New York. Like anyone would bat an eye.

At the next red light, Madison grabbed her earbud and tapped the third favorite on her phone. After two and a half rings, her father picked up.

"Hello? Frankie?"

His voice made her smile, and the nickname pulled her right back to the simpler time of being his little girl. "Hi, Dad."

"Is everything okay?"

A twinge of guilt hit her when she realized it had been some time since they'd last spoken. The day she arrived in New York, in fact. "Yeah, Dad. Everything's fine. I was just thinking that it might be nice to drop by and catch up sometime."

"Jellybean, that would be great. When are you thinking?"

"Well, I need to check something, but is tomorrow too soon? Would that be all right?"

"Of course. I'd love it, but don't you have to work?"

Typical Dad. Worrying about the big city swallowing his little girl whole. And probably wondering if she might be on her way to moving back home.

"Well, in a way, this might end up being for work. It's hard to explain. I'll call you tomorrow morning with the details."

"Sure," he said cheerfully. "Anytime. I'll always be here for you."

You, and another guy I know.

After extending the silence with a smile, she heard, "Frankie? Did I lose you?"

"Still here, Dad. Can I ask you something? Years ago, was there a guy you helped out through a tough time?"

"Well, that might be a long list," her father said with a sigh. "Our vets are a tough lot, but under the right pressure, even the toughest steel will fracture and break."

Carefully, Madison considered her words, not wanting to tip her hand. If she were too eager, he'd see right through her. And this wasn't the time to bring up her relationship status.

"Maybe this will help. The guy I'm asking about wasn't a vet, but might have been wounded. In combat." She paused, thoughtful in considering the scab she might be scratching at. "It was someone who . . . knew Jack. Was with Jack . . . on his last assignment."

Now it was her dad's turn to stretch out the silence. She could feel him holding back. But whether it led to something would be his call, not hers.

Finally, he spoke. "I think you might mean AJ."

"No, it's—"

Wait. Another puzzle piece fell into place from back when Madison first started working at DGI. What was that the name G.I. Joe had mentioned when Alex rescued him from some thugs on the sidewalk outside their headquarters? *AJ and I are gonna catch up*, the homeless man had said.

"Yes. AJ. That's him. Can you tell me about AJ?"

∼

"Frankie," her father said once he'd finished his story, "I can't wait to see you. Love you, honey."

"Love you too, Dad."

With the call disconnected and her destination approaching, Madison checked overhead, scanning the Homelink panels and pressing a button. Nothing happened. When she pressed a second button, the large door directly ahead of her rolled upward, welcoming her. Her smile beamed as she rolled into the familiar penthouse garage.

Just counting the cars parked there wasn't a foolproof way to know for sure if Alex was home. Six cars, spaciously parked throughout, didn't always mean he was there. He'd call for a car service more often than not so he could work during his commute, making the most of every hour of the day.

She pulled the access card from her purse. Though she'd used it that very morning, the rigid edges felt different in her hand. A few hours ago, she was on her way back here to return this card to Alex—ready for one last visit with the sole purpose of leaving it all behind, including their relationship.

And now? Now everything had changed.

When the elevator rose and then opened to the penthouse, the luxury apartment felt warmer, strangely calming and yet energizing her all at once. The feeling surrounded her, wrapping her in a sweet comfort and familiarity. She was home.

"Paco, I'm in the office."

Madison's pulse kicked up at the sound of Alex's voice, and she hurried down the hall, her plush panda slippers muffling her steps. Stepping inside his office, she found him deep in thought, studying two of his three desk screens. He hadn't heard her enter.

Clearing her throat, she said, "It's not Paco."

In an instant, Alex jumped from his chair and rushed over, stopping short of a sweeping embrace as he noticed her head-to-toe ensemble.

"Madison. I'm . . ." He hesitated, taking all of her in.

"Not a word," she said, pointing a solemn finger straight at his nose.

Crossing his arms, Alex released a hand to smother his lips, keeping his remarks—and chuckle—to himself.

Smart man.

"Good. Now it's your turn to not say anything and just listen." She took in a needed breath, settling the butterflies fluttering in her stomach, holding them still before setting them free. "I know you think all of this could have been avoided if you'd just told me everything to begin with. And I get it. It's complicated . . . maybe more complicated than even you realize." Her remark barely scratched the surface of so many things, including Paco's confession.

Daring to take a step closer, Alex smiled, his eyes bright with hope.

"But *I'm* not ready to make it uncomplicated. At least, not if that means DGI continues without you. A dirtbag like Frank Seaver can't buy me, and I would hope to God he couldn't buy you either." Madison pulled down the large hand covering Alex's mouth and tightened both her hands around it. "Please tell me I'm right."

His other hand caressed her cheek, stroking her face as his

eyes drank her in. "You're right," he whispered to her lips before pressing a kiss there, lightly at first. Then he deepened the kiss, running his hands through her hair and across her back, pausing to pull away just enough to press his forehead to hers.

"I thought I'd lost you," he said softly, and their lips met again.

Her body relaxed into his. "I thought I'd lost myself. I didn't trust you because I didn't trust myself, or my own instincts. Instead, I believed a slimeball like Frank Seaver, even though I knew he was manipulating me." Cringing, Madison became furious all over again at the thought of letting a contemptable puppet-master rope her in. "I hate that a schemer like Frank Seaver swayed me so easily. Especially after that scumbag nearly cost me my interview with DGI."

Alex's brows drew together. "What do you mean?"

"The morning I arrived for my interview, we had a full-body slam into each other. The bastard spilled his coffee all over me —*spiked* coffee. Left me smelling like an Irish pub."

With a deep sigh, Alex dropped his head. "You, uh, don't say."

"I had to go into the executive suites of DGI with no blouse on under my blazer, just my camisole . . . *and* interview with Gina. I'm sure you can imagine how that went."

"Oh, I can picture it. I mean, I can imagine your frustration."

With his head down, he led her to sit on the contemporary settee. Surprised, Madison watched as he moved away from her, opting for a seat on the corner chair to her side. They were seated face-to-face.

"I honestly can't believe I got the job after that." Rather than let her emotions run wild, she caught the angst in Alex's face. His expression was twisted. Tortured. She reached over to stroke his chest. "Sorry. I didn't mean to dredge up more."

"No, it's not that." Regret seemed to fill his eyes, and his clenched jaw worried her. Pulling away, he clasped his hands and steepled his fingers toward her. "Madison, remember I asked if you remembered our first encounter?"

Nodding, she hated admitting it. "Yes. And I still don't."

With a hand on her knee and releasing a deep breath, he looked her straight in the eyes. "Seaver didn't spill the coffee on you. I did."

"You did?" Madison wrinkled her nose, hardly believing him, but Alex persisted.

"Yes, me. Me and my dark roast and Woodford."

As more of his explanation spilled out, Madison hung on his every guilty word.

"I was edgy and irritated that morning when my car didn't show up." Stopping himself, he came clean. "But the truth is, I was an asshole of epic proportions because..."

"Because what?" Madison wasn't letting the moment slip by without the truth. All of it. "Whatever it is you've been keeping bottled up, it's time. Time to let everything go."

Lacing his fingers, gripping so tightly his knuckles turned white, Alex continued. "I had a hard time dealing with the past, Madison. And sometimes, I—I still have a hard time. There are days when everything crashes in around me, all at once with no warning. I don't handle it well, so I just escape. Get away. As far away from anyone and everyone as I can."

"You self-isolate," Madison said, clarifying with a term she knew all too well.

"Yes," he said quietly. "Anyway, that morning, I could feel it coming on. Taking over. I tried the spiked coffee to take the edge off, and when it didn't work, I tried getting away."

Gently, she reached for his hand to comfort him and he took it, sandwiching it between both of his, as if desperate to keep her there. She dipped her chin, nudging him with her eyes to continue.

"I didn't see you," Alex said softly. "You were right in front of me. And I know this will sound crazy—or crazier—but I kept feeling like you were coming. Like I needed to look out for you. Because maybe we would just, well, bump into each other."

He paused, noticing her playful squint.

Did he really just say that?

"The point is, I had you. Right there under my goddamned nose like you were gift-wrapped and hand delivered by heaven itself, and what did I do? I doused you in coffee and booze, berated you, and stormed off."

Taunting him, she said, "I believe your exact words were 'watch where you're going.'"

Smirking, Alex took the ribbing. "That sounds about right. And I believe you astutely singled me out as a jack-hole. A jack-hole who nearly lost you."

His expression wasn't just apologetic. Madison could see he was more than just sorry. He was tortured.

"And today," he said, "I nearly lost you again, and all because I didn't tell you everything up front. Madison, I'm so sorry. I swear I'll never keep anything from you again."

But she was only half listening, readily forgiving him more than it seemed he might ever forgive himself. Her mind wandering for a moment, she fixated on his words, the ones he'd just said a moment ago.

I called him a jack-hole, but how did he know?

Curiosity piqued, she was ready to pull the curtains all the way back and completely expose this Wizard of Igz. "You know, I've spent a lot of time wondering how a girl like me was lucky enough to land a job like this. I mean, maybe I wasn't exactly *un*qualified, but I was definitely *under*qualified. Gina said as much. And I walked in dressed to audition for office floozy number two. On top of which, I told the VP of human capital that I wanted to shove my heel up her executive butt. And yet I was hired. On the spot. Or technically, on the spot my ass fell on in the lobby. You didn't have something to do with that, did you, Mr. Drake?"

He nodded, giving her a boyish grin that always brought out those sexy dimples.

Serious and businesslike, Madison stood. The consummate gentleman, Alex tried to stand as well, but she placed her hand on his shoulder to urge him to sit and stay.

She didn't release her touch until he relaxed all the way back in his seat. Pacing, Madison pieced together the puzzle. The one hidden in plain sight. The one she'd struggled with for so long was now evident and clear.

"The shoes!" she blurted. "Those gorgeous shoes you bought me. You knew about my broken heel because"—she studied him, eager to see the truth reflect back in his eyes—"you saw my heel break. There's a camera in Gina's office, isn't there?"

"Actually, there are three." When Madison froze her pacing, fidgeting uncomfortably and tugging at her collar, Alex quickly explained. "Gina insisted. We've had a few disgruntled employees in the past, and in case anything happened as a result, she wanted to ensure she could capture everything on video. They're in the corners of the ceiling, in full view."

Mentally sorting through the memories of the day she interviewed at DGI, Madison locked another piece in place. "And when I was making my, well, illustrious escape, Gina's phone rang. I thought it was security, but it was you. *You* hired me."

"I heard you tell Gina off. I heard every word of you describing my deplorable behavior. I had to make it right."

Of all things, that tidbit actually took Madison by surprise. "So, you didn't hire me because I was Jack's sister?"

Alex shook his head. "It wasn't until Gina called out your name after I told her to hire you that I realized you might be Jack's sister. I even asked Paco to check it out, but he literally took forever. Like he was *trying* to blow me off."

Madison turned away, masking any insider knowledge of Paco's guilt.

"He didn't confirm my suspicion until after our first night together, when I asked him to look after you that morning. Madison, from the way you stood up to Gina, and protecting Joe from those thugs, and even standing up to me when you thought I might hurt him, *you* were the woman I've been waiting for, Jack's sister or not. The whole month I was traveling after that, I couldn't stop thinking of you. I've been trying to figure out how to tell you. About the coffee. And the gifts. And Jack. I thought that if you got to know me better, good and bad, you'd have more insight. A better understanding because, well . . ."

Together, they said in unison, "It's complicated."

Nodding, Madison imagined how the awkward conversation might have played out.

Hi, I spilled coffee on you and was a total d-bag about it, so I hired you to make it good. And, by the way, I was in that whole explosion that killed your brother, Jack, but had nothing to do with it. At all. And it has nothing to do with why I'm chasing you.

"Best-case scenario," Alex said, "it would be a remarkable meet-cute story that no one but our closest friends would believe. And worst case, I'd get to hold you a little longer before . . ." He shrugged, unable to finish the sentence, then his eyes met hers.

"But, Madison, before you make up your mind, you have a right to know all of it." White-knuckled again from squeezing his clasped hands, he huffed out a breath. "There are times when I'm not okay. And I don't just get okay. I have a really hard time dealing with things. But I will deal with it. Shield you from all of it."

Her heart swelled, and a wry smile formed at his impossible offer. *He always needs to protect me.*

"Shield me?" she asked. "So you can continue hiding this part of your life and how deeply it affects you, even though it is your life? Is that what you were doing at Jess and Mark's place? Let's pretend nothing was wrong, even though you hurled your phone halfway across the property?" Gently, she exposed him, as if he were a kid denying tasting a chocolate cake, though his lips were slathered in frosting. "Tell me who you were calling, and know that whatever you tell me, this is our safe space. We can tell each other anything."

His lips formed a wry grin. "Mark."

But his calling Mark didn't make any sense. Mark was close by at the time, in the other room. When she frowned at Alex in confusion, he answered her unasked questions.

"I didn't know how bad the attack would be and I couldn't move. If he picked up, all I'd have to say is *get Madison*, and he would've discreetly found a reason to get you out of there. Just until I rode out the wave."

"You mean ride it out alone. You think I don't see it? Don't see you? Alex, you run at midnight. Push paperwork until three a.m. You can't shield me from every side of you, and I wouldn't want you to."

"But, Madison—"

She held up a hand. "Alex, I need you to stop trying to protect me for a moment and listen. After Jack died and my parents divorced, my anxiety was out of control. Everything set me off, so the doctors put me on meds. My mom thought it would help. Help me sleep. And eat. And be around people. And breathe. Because God forbid I deal with what I was feeling. So, I tried to hide it. The meds. The anxiety. *Me.* I became invisible in my own life. I didn't let anyone know, not even my dad, because I figured it was my issue to deal with."

Shutting her eyes, she wrapped her arms around herself. "The only thing that got me off the meds was joining the track team in high school. Running isolated me. Gave me precious seconds away from the unrelenting feelings that were just around every corner, ready to swallow me whole. I found a way to keep up with the heart that always threatened to pound right out of my chest."

With a small smile, she shrugged. "I still break out in hives every now and again, and I still work out when my pulse jumps ahead of me. Is that something you want me to hide from you,

Alex? If you're part of my life, should I deal with it all on my own?"

"No. God, no. Madison, I'll always be by your side. I'm not going anywhere."

She moved in front of him, her tone reassuring. "Then why on earth would you expect any different of me? And by the way, *I'm* not going anywhere. You might be the guy who was a total ass to me . . ." Alex turned his head away, but she kept going. "But you're also the guy who gave me a chance at a remarkable job, rescued me from a pretty scary situation from three nutjobs on the street, and cared for me like no one ever has."

Madison leaned over to cup the scruffy angles of his jaw, encouraging his eyes to meet hers. "And you might *not* be the guy who was able to save Jack's life," she said, sniffing back a tear. "But make no mistake, Alex, I know you're the guy who nearly died trying." She pressed a soft kiss on his mouth, whispering to his lips, "Like I said, I'm not going anywhere."

With that, he stood, looking down at her and pulling her near. But an attempt at a tight embrace was stopped by the palm of her hand planted firmly against the solid muscles of his chest.

"Oh, you're not off the hook just yet," she said with a scolding tone, ready to toss him one fiery coal of a question to blaze a trail far away from the past.

Spreading his arms out wide, he waited. "What do you need?" he asked, his deep tone sending heat straight to her core.

Licking her lips, Madison stepped back. "I've been replaying what happened that day. The day we met. Our little meet-cute over coffee."

His posture tense, he stood tall, as if ready for whatever punishment she had ready.

Come on, Alex. Smile.

She kept going. "Something about it is really making me wonder. Tell me something, Mr. Drake . . ."

He swallowed hard. "Anything, Ms. Taylor."

Toe-to-toe, she stared up at him. Businesslike and arms crossed, she gave him just a glimpse of a bewitching smile.

"If you hadn't spilled the coffee on me, and I'd been wearing my button-up-to-my-neck blouse beneath that blazer when I was interviewed by Gina, and had my hair up and away from my face, similar to how it is now, would you have been watching so intently, hanging on my every, um, word?"

Between the arch of Madison's eyebrow and her suggestive tone, he relaxed his stance, finally caving with a boyish grin when he realized she was toying with him, daring him to join her game.

"Why, Ms. Taylor," Alex said with a mild amount of indignity as he took a few leisurely steps behind her. The heat of his hands worked across her shoulders and down her arms. Her shiver was instant.

His hands made their way to her wrists, unlocking her arms. She melted into him as he worked to slide off her robe. "You could have been wearing anything. Blouse. No blouse. Adorable *E.T.* T-shirt."

Carefully, Alex tugged at her scrunchie, releasing her wavy locks. Fingering her tresses free, he loosened her cascade of waves down her neck, laying the tendrils gently across her heaving chest. His tone was low in her ear.

"You could have had your hair in any style. Up, down, French twist, chignon," which he said with a perfect French accent, and turned her in his arms.

She peeked up at him through her eyelashes, welcoming his seduction.

"No matter how you looked, I have every confidence that, like now, I wouldn't have been able to take my eyes off you." His fingers lifted her chin, and his mouth melted over hers, pressing lightly on her lips. "But," he said with a serious and discerning glance, "for the record, the blazer *sans* blouse will forever be a fan favorite."

Smiling, Madison welcomed another kiss, parting her lips and letting Alex explore deeper with sweeps of his tongue. His strong arms embraced her, lifting her so her legs could wrap around his hips and waist. Relaxed in his hold, she rested easily on his hands, and he tightened his hold under each cheek.

His lips never left hers as they made their way to the bedroom. Once there, he set her on the bed, soaking in every bit of her in his hungry gaze, panda slippers and all.

When he reached for his tie, Madison stopped him, letting him loosen the knot but not fully release it. "Hang on. You got my runway best. How about yours?"

Leaning down, Alex rested both hands on the mattress, caging her between them. Growling, he lightly grazed his lips against hers. "And just what did you have in mind?"

Button by button, she unfastened his shirt, then tugged it loose from his slacks as he helped, unclipping the cuffs. Peeling the tailored shirt from his skin, she finished with one final move. Drawing the collar down through the inside of the tie, she managed to slip it off without disturbing anything else. The only thing covering any part of his ripped upper body was his GG bees silk tie.

Suggestively, Madison tightened the knot back up to his neck, slipping a finger along the line of the dip in his collar bone, then leaned back, fully admiring her masterpiece. "There. Now there's a fan favorite."

Not the least bit shy, Alex looked down, impressed with her work. He returned his gaze to hers. "How about I keep on mine if you keep on yours," he said, eyeing a T-shirt that had to be wonderfully tight for the occasion. "I mean, it really is one of my favorite movies. You know, it inspired the song 'Heartlight' by Neil Diamond."

Could he be any more perfect?

"You don't say?" Tugging his tie like a silk leash, she summoned another kiss.

Alex was everything. Tender and sweet. Frisky and fun. And

maybe a first for both of them, free. Free of any fears or doubts, there were no walls between them, no secrets holding them back. Together, they could cherish and adore each other for the beautifully imperfect people they were.

"Lie back," Alex said softly, quickly removing the rest of his clothes, then kneeling before her.

He removed her slippers, then slowly massaged his hands up her knees and past her thighs. Hooking his fingers into the waistband, he took off her pajama bottoms, laying a trail of hot kisses across her skin before returning her slippers to her feet. She lifted her head, squinting at him with a look of pure suspicion.

Climbing on top of her, he said quietly, "There. Now you'll be snug and comfy while I get snug and comfy."

Her giggles melted as his mouth crashed onto hers. The slightest parting of her lips willingly invited his tongue in, and her hips began to rock, riding the solid thigh that pressed against her core.

A few hot kisses landed on Madison's neck, open-mouthed ones that grazed along the thin fabric of her shirt as he lifted it to bare her breast. Massaging its weight in his hand, Alex teased her, circling his fingertip along her nipple.

It was agony, and she needed more. Brushing his lips along one nipple, he plucked the other. Her back arched, and his teeth unleashed one terse pull before releasing her breast and inciting a moan.

Lazily, he skimmed a finger across the plane of her stomach before skating it along the inside of her thigh. Madison ached for him. Needed him. Begged with her body as she spread her knees wider, needing him more with each touch.

Alex breezed his fingers softly across her wet pussy, dipping them in just enough to coat his finger with her wetness. He ran the finger across her mouth, then licked. Their kiss was intoxicating. Tasting him as she tasted herself.

With her legs spread wide, his fingers once again painted her slickness across her folds before plunging deep inside, fucking her in long strokes before pulling away. Beneath heavy lids, she watched. Alex sucked each finger clean, enjoying every bit of her flavor.

Desperate, she leaned over, kissing him and pressing him to his back. Swinging her leg over, she climbed on top of him, needing all of him deep inside her. Rubbing herself against the length of his cock, she moaned at the sensation before trying to take him in.

"Shhh, not yet." He groaned, reaching for the nightstand to retrieve a condom from the drawer, and tore it open.

Madison snatched it from his hand and tossed it aside, lowering herself. The swollen tip of him held a bead of pre-cum she had to lick. Stroking his shaft, her tongue crossed the head before swallowing him clear to her throat.

Falling back, Alex said, "Yes, Madison. God, yes." He stroked her hair, and she let him move her head in all the ways he needed.

She took her time, sucking him hard, then pulling back to sweep her tongue along the smooth round tip. Her rhythm picked up, sucking and releasing, and she watched as Alex took her in, staring back at her.

"Wait," he said in a low voice, gruff in his plea.

She rocked her head up and down the length of his shaft before taking one last circling lick. Then she took a second to sheath him and take in his size before inching her body in place.

His strong hands grabbed her hips, holding her still as he forced all of himself in at once, stretching her wide. Gripping her ass, he rocked her, watching her body move as he thrust up into her, completely making her his.

Alex's thumb rubbed her mouth, brushing the fullness of her lower lip before sliding inside. "Suck, Madison."

She did, not losing the rhythm of riding him. Slowly, he pulled his thumb from her lips and place the ball of it on her clit, rubbing in circles as she increased her pace. She was on the edge. But watching him, so was he.

"More," she begged.

Still inside her, he flipped her to her back. Wildly bucking, he filled her as she cried out. Slowing, he pulled out only to the tip, then thrust firmly in to the hilt before fucking her hard and senseless.

Panting, Madison cried out, "Please, don't stop."

"Your wish is definitely my command."

Alex did this over and over. Driving her to the brink, slowing, then dragging his length out, only to force himself back in and fuck her until her body exploded in a thousand pulses of pleasure, collapsing on his thickness in crushing waves. Her cries weren't the only ones filling the room, and the climax that ripped her apart was fueled by his, filling her with a heat she could feel deep within.

Dizzy and drained, he dropped his head next to hers, and his lips nuzzled her ear. His breaths were labored and heavy, leaving him fighting to speak. Breathlessly, he said, "I love you, Madison."

Stroking his hair, Madison took in a long, lingering whiff of his scent. "I love you too," she said, tightening her legs around him.

∽

Comforted in being spooned by Alex, Madison lay there exhausted but awake. Somehow, the tip of his tie rested on her arm, where his finger lazily stroked. She remained in her T-shirt, not minding the question it raised.

"Madison E. Taylor, right?" he asked.

She grinned but was content to keep her back pressed into him, avoiding his eyes.

"Madison E.T.? Is that why Jack got the shirt for you?"

"Mm-hmm. How did you know my middle initial?"

"Oh, I have my ways." His voice lowered to a whisper. "It's discreetly hidden on the back of your access card. And on your license. And on the employee roster. And listed on your Skype profile." He chuckled into her shoulder, then nibbled it. His voice regained its soft volume. "What's the E stand for?"

Madison gazed into the darkness. "Nothing special. Just a name." She pulled his hand into hers, weaving their fingers together. "Alex, I'd like to take you somewhere tomorrow. Is your calendar really free?"

He pulled her hand up, giving it a long kiss. "Yes," he growled low, letting his lips linger on her knuckles.

She glanced back, craning her neck to look at him. "I ask because it might take the whole day. Maybe even pour into the next one."

He rolled her back toward him and looked down on her, his gaze soft and sincere. "It can take the whole year." His lips found hers. "I'm all yours, Madison Taylor. Completely and forever yours."

They lay there, holding each other for the rest of the night.

Though Alex dozed off, Madison was energized, preoccupied with ideas. She stayed awake most of the night, her feet kicked out just enough from beneath the covers to expose the panda slippers still on her feet. She only nodded off after working out the details of a plan.

CHAPTER 22

ALEX

Alex awakened, reaching for Madison. Instead, he found a note. He grabbed it, but then slid his hand between the comforter and the bed, finding it just warm enough to mean she'd left about half an hour ago. He rubbed the sleep from his eyes and read the delicate print.

> *Take your time getting up.*
> *Coffee when you're ready.*
> *Big day. No hints.*

He rolled to her side of the bed, pulling in a long breath of her scent. A faint hint of her perfume and shampoo blended with the seductive aroma of her body, and that delicious smell of sex. With another deep inhale, he moaned. Rolling back, he thought of last night.

Before he could get too lost in remembering each of her delectable curves, the faintest whiff of coffee hit him. Alex yawned, then propped up on his elbows.

At the end of the bed, he could see Tom Ford jeans and an Armani navy T-shirt had been laid out. *When was my last casual day?* With nothing at all coming to mind, he savored the thrill of unpredictability.

No hints, huh? I love a challenge.

Strolling through the penthouse wearing nothing but a smile and the gold-accented tie, Alex strutted straight to the kitchen. Straightening his tie, he decided to make himself more presentable. He cleared his throat, then entered.

Madison whirled around, admiring him with a giggle. He let her eyes roam across his head-to-toe fashion statement. Giving her his best *GQ* pose, he adjusted an invisible cuff. "Good morning, Ms. Taylor. I heard coffee was up for grabs. Tell me, is there a dress code?"

Madison, in her white peasant blouse and denim stretch capris, brought her oversize mug of cappuccino to her lips. "Oh, you've met it." She took her sip with another hungry glance up and down. Then, with a whimsical frothy moustache, she asked, "Espresso?"

"Please," Alex said, stepping closer to kiss off the foam.

She started the machine, then straightened his tie before handing him the saucer and cup. He sipped it slowly, leaning a hand on the bright Calacatta marble, enjoying the views that baked in a sun-filled metropolitan morning. He stood every bit as dignified as if fully suited up for work.

"If you entered DGI as is," she said playfully, "would anyone tell the emperor he had no clothes?"

Considering her question, he said, "They might not, but I'm pretty sure their lawyers would." Still gazing at the view, he asked, "No hints, huh?"

"No hints," Madison said, her businesslike tone conveying the staunchness of her position, while mimicking his nonchalant *always the CEO* demeanor. She stared out the window too, enjoying another long sip of her nearly empty drink.

Alex's gaze moved from the window to meet hers, which

darted to the arrival of his morning wood. "At least tell me if it's in the city or not."

Setting her cup aside, she went in for a long, tender kiss, welcoming every muscle of his nude embrace. Peering at him through deceptive come-hither lashes, the girl held her ground.

"Not one single hint, Mr. Drake." Madison looked down, admiring the skyscraper nestled longingly between them. "And as much as I'd like you to poke and prod it out of me, I'm sorry to say we really, *really* don't have time for that."

Apologetically, she looked up. "I'll start your shower," she said, giving him one final kiss before heading to the master bath.

With a heavy sigh, Alex leaned over, ready to place his cup in the sink, Yelping, he glared at the Calacatta marble giving him freezer burn as it tried to prove it was harder than him. He scowled at the counter.

This is not a competition.

CHAPTER 23

MADISON

While Alex enjoyed a leisurely shower, Madison made a call.

"Hello, Miss Madison." The usually upbeat Latin accent sounded ever so slightly annoyed, probably due to her helping herself to his Lambo. "If this is payback for the earrings, I'm pretty sure I did *not* say you could have my car."

Madison played it off. "Are you *sure*? How much can one really remember when they were three sheets to the wind?" His silence was a blaring broadcast of the doubt in his mind. Madison only let it linger a moment before fessing up. "Don't worry. You didn't give me your car. I'm just borrowing it."

"Well, at least you took it to Alex's." When Madison didn't respond, he said, "And no, that's not mind reading. I have a tracker." He paused, then added, "But never mind. Keep it."

Madison's own doubts tapped her shoulder. "That's generous. And crazy. Are you still drinking?"

He chuckled. "No, Miss Madison, I'm not still drinking."

A new set of ringtones announced his request to take the call to FaceTime. Smiling, she accepted.

Paco had his face fill the frame, like ear to ear. Glaring at her, he popped that ridiculously adorable raised eyebrow. The one that always meant he was far from mad.

Bursting with laughter, Madison faked her own knowing squint, and he finally moved the phone to pan out the view.

At first, she assumed he was just proving his sobriety by looking fresh as a daisy, sporting a sharp new suit, pressed pocket square, and those gorgeous diamond earrings. But then his stolid expression melted into an overflowing grin as he swayed just out of the shot. The camera caught the unmistakable logo of a gold-on-black charging bull.

"Pull back," he said to whomever held his phone. His impromptu cameraman did so, showcasing Paco prominently seated on the hood of a Rosso Mars red Aventador. "Like I said, keep it."

Delighted, Madison let out a loud squeal. "Really?"

Paco pulled the letter she'd left him from his interior breast pocket, giving it a pageant wave before the screen. "Really, Miss Madison," he said, his voice low and compelling.

She'd given him a meaningful gift. He was clearly tagging her back. He took his phone back from the attendant, and she heard him request a little privacy.

But she couldn't wait any longer before addressing a serious issue with the man. "Paco, seeing as you're the only brother-in-law I'll ever have, how about you just call me Madison?"

Rather than respond, he simply gaped at her with a beaming grin and a few appreciative blinks.

"Is that a yes?"

He nodded. "Yes," he said, returning the letter to his inside pocket, and patted his blazer at his heart. "Okay, *Madison*. Yes, really. That car is my gift to you. Plus, you need an excuse to wear those badass gloves."

"Well, you giving me this car is kind of fortuitous, and keeps me from having to ask for an extended loan. But I do still need a favor."

"For my favorite *hermanita*, anything."

Hermanita. Madison knew the term of endearment from ninth-grade Spanish. Her heart melted at the word. *Little sister*. It hit her then, how she missed being a sister.

"So, what wicked scheme shall we be partners in crime on?"

CHAPTER 24

ALEX

Alex strolled out from the bedroom, comfortable in his shirt and jeans. Though the lines naturally showcased the prominent cuts and curves of his chiseled build, everything still hung loose enough to make the outfit freeing.

His hair, still damp from the shower, was the extent of the effort he'd make in his appearance, giving it a quick comb-through with his fingers. And his scruff could use an extra day to grow out. Why not? No meetings. No work. His executive staff got the memo he'd sent them, so not a single email or voice mail waited on his phone. Nothing was on fire. No one needed his undivided attention. No one but Madison.

What's she got planned?

He found her packing his things in an overnight bag. "Don't forget my Speedo," he joked.

As he approached her, open-armed and ready for an embrace, she greeted him with, of all things, his portfolio. "I know you're not used to being away from work, so I printed out a few things, just in case you need something to pass the time."

Disappointed, he took it, overstuffed with hours' worth of

paperwork. He thumbed through it. "Um, exactly how far are we going?"

"Just far enough. And I'm driving. The rest of the luggage is already in the car."

Alex scanned the documents as the elevator carried them down to the garage, and, of course, several items screamed for his attention. So much so, he barely noticed the car they got into.

A bright stream of daylight hit him as the garage door opened, forcing him to squint. He scanned the car. No sunglasses.

Wait, whose car is this?

"Here," Madison said, handing him a pair.

"Thanks," he said, now even more suspicious as he checked out her instant ease behind the wheel. Ready to give her a few pointers, he was surprised as she powered on, revved the engine, and slammed the pedal to the metal, swiftly carrying them off.

Nothing like pulling some early morning Gs to wake you up.

Her overpowering acceleration whipped him full force back into the seat, bringing a wide smile to his face. "So you like fast cars, beautiful? I'll keep that in mind. Paco's car?"

Demurely, Madison smiled at him. "No."

Alex scanned the interior of the car, then slid his butt around in place, as if waxing the seat with his ass. "Well, I'm pretty sure my butt has a permanent imprint in this seat. It's remarkably molded to my shape."

Shifting his motion to thrust back and forth, his little hump fest pushed Madison's restraint to a full-blown laugh. "I don't know what to tell you. It's not Paco's car."

Dumbfounded at her attempt at deception, Alex decided to turn up the heat. Despite the hard stare he laid on her, her expression remained stoic. Even as he leaned over, growled against her neck, and asked, "Not Paco's car, huh?" she didn't crack.

With his gaze firmly on her, he popped open the glove box

he'd opened a time or two before. Without looking, he fished out the contents.

Hooking the fuzzy handcuffs with his finger, he dangled them next to her face. "And these, Ms. Taylor? Are these for later when I've been very, very bad?" His voice was deep and scolding.

Busted, Madison cracked a smile, crumpling under the pressure. "Okay, okay. The car isn't Paco's because he—well, he gave it to me. It's mine now." She then circled a finger at the cuffs on prominent display. "But *those* are not."

Alex slumped a little in his seat, flipping through a wide range of possibilities that could have led to this.

Paco handed over his Big Banana to Madison? Color me impressed and confused. But at least it explains the charge from Paco's favorite Lamborghini dealer.

"Well, you must have given him something *extremely* valuable in return."

Patiently, Alex waited for her to reply, but was met with her tight pouty lips and a poker face fixed diligently on the road ahead. Sure, he could press her further, but instead, he sat and plotted, knowing he'd eventually get to the bottom of it. Hopefully, she'd resist. Handcuffs around her sexy little wrists would be an interrogation well worth the wait.

"All I can say," he said, "is if Paco gave you this car but not these," he clapped the cuffs together before tossing them back into the glove compartment, "then we seriously need to work on your negotiating skills."

Madison's smile widened as she looked over, but he didn't look back, instead opting to bury his nose in an insane pile of work.

Alex pulled up one document, scrutinizing it like a page from the *Wall Street Journal* while using his free hand to take Madison's from the task of steering. Planting a firm kiss on it, he brushed his lips over her knuckles for a second before returning it to the job of handling this beast of a car.

She accelerated a little more, and Alex ignored a small, unsettled voice inside his head that told him something was brewing. Something big. And good or bad, he could sense it. Whatever *it* was, it was present and powerful, and he suspected it would change everything.

CHAPTER 25

ALEX

As the three-hour drive breezed by, Alex couldn't resist a quick dive into DGI's latest quarterly projections. Something about the hum of this car and the portfolio on his lap always flipped him to full-on work mode.

He only asked Madison *where are we going?* and *are we almost there?* a few times before easing back into the passion that kept him sane all those years. Work.

But as the car slowed, Alex looked up and took in the quaint country road they were now traveling. Something seemed familiar. The houses were close enough to each other to be considered a neighborhood, but were far from being on top of each other. The modest homes were spaced out on large, tree-filled lots, where the residents enjoyed privacy but not solitude.

As soon as Madison cut the engine, Alex paid closer attention to one house in particular. It was sweet and alive with spring flowers and a variety of birds flitting to and from feeders in the yard, each hung at the best vantage point from nearby windows to give any onlookers a glimpse at birdwatching.

He remembered. Cardinals. Bluebirds. But mostly sparrows. The little birds that had given him fleeting moments of thinking about something other than his pain. Or the past. Instead, he'd just watched them fly free.

Stunned, he turned to Madison, who'd already exited the car. A small grin emerged as he focused on just one thing. "Dan?" Opening his door, he slowly climbed out of the car. Dazed, he took a few steps forward and grabbed her hand.

"You okay?" she asked, a small trace of worry in her words.

"Madison, how—" He stopped short, realizing the answer. "Paco." He took another look at the house he hadn't seen since... "Are you sure you want to do this?"

"Don't worry. I'm sure."

Alex took a single, contemplative breath. Then, without warning, he whisked her away, yanking her hand to tow her around the side of the house. Moving stealthily and damn near in a belly crawl, he led her to the edge of the back porch. She had to think he was a psychopath, but he knew what he was doing.

Looking left, then right, he pressed his back against the wall, and held Madison back as well, as if hiding from an enemy's sights. Poking his head around the corner, he examined the yard. It was well-maintained with several Adirondack chairs, one with a fresh bottle of beer saturated in condensation. It was the perfect cold drink for a warm day, and had only recently been abandoned.

"What are you doing?" she whispered, giving him a concerned look.

Ready to explain his bizarre tactical movements, he froze. The unmistakable cocking of a single-action pistol cracked the air. The barrel was pressed to the side of Alex's head, prompting him to hold up both hands.

"I'll tell you what he's doing," the booming voice announced. "He's making himself at home." The gruff man uncocked the gun and placed it on a nearby table, where two more ice-cold beers waited. "Welcome home, *both* of you."

Madison took Alex's hand, tightly clinging to it while

swinging around to give her dad a big bear hug. "So, you two *do* know each other." Spotting the beers, she released Alex and headed over to the waiting bottles.

Dan gave Alex a good once-over. "Well, it's been half a second, but I reckon I'd spot AJ just about anywhere." Her father slapped Alex's open hand, shaking it hard. "How've you been, son?"

"Better," Alex said, pausing as if to add *I think*. He broke their handshake to remove his sunglasses and hang them from the neck of his shirt. Uncertain, he met Dan's gaze. "A lot better since . . ."

Alex hesitated, suddenly concerned how Dan would feel about him and Madison. Dan was one of the few people who knew the shape, size, and weight of every skeleton in Alex's closet. That, and it had been nearly a decade since they'd seen each other. He had to have doubts. What sane man wouldn't have doubts about a loose cannon like Alex Drake dating his daughter?

"Good!" Dan patted his shoulder. "You being better is very good."

His expression was so warm and approving that Alex shook his hand again, at which point Dan pulled him into a bear hug that Alex couldn't help but reciprocate.

"Thanks, Dan."

"No need to thank me. You did all the heavy lifting."

"Well, at least for the beer, if I can pry one away from your girl there."

Madison held it at arm's length, teasing Alex with it while making her way to the chairs on the lawn. Eagerly, she kicked off her shoes so she could wiggle her toes in the freshly trimmed blades of grass. Alex followed suit, unable to remember the last time he'd felt the simple joy of bare feet on the ground.

Madison handed Alex his untouched bottle before plopping her butt in one of the chairs. She was looking at them both with a fascinated smile as her gaze moved from Alex to her father. "I still can't figure out how I had no idea that you two knew each other."

Dan and Alex exchanged glances, silently debating who would start. Finally, Dan jumped in.

"Well, after the divorce, your mom took you away. You needed stability, and I was, well, really messed up after we lost Jack."

An apology clearly on her tongue, Madison grabbed his hand, but her father squeezed it quickly, then waved off what she was about to say.

"No, Frankie, your mom was right. Saying I had a tough time coping is like saying a tornado is a stiff breeze. I needed to deal with my shit without dragging you down with me. I needed to be alone. At least, I thought I did. And then I met AJ. I didn't think anyone could be more messed up than me." He took a swig of the cold beer, giving Alex an unsettled glance. "Boy, was I wrong."

Alex drew in a breath. "I returned to the States with just one thing on my mind. Returning the book and photo. I never felt right about having them. After all, Jack had a family. I figured it was the least I could do."

Dan glared, shaking a finger at Alex before correcting him. "Hey, if you're gonna tell this story, don't gloss over the nitty-gritty details." He turned to Madison. "The guy who showed up on my doorstep wasn't exactly *released* from the hospital."

When Madison glanced at Alex, he shrugged with a guilty smirk. "Okay, okay. I left the hospital a little early, but I hated taking up a bed with all the injured vets around me. I felt like, I don't know . . . a fraud. I wasn't active duty, and I was *technically* stable, so they couldn't keep me. I caught the next plane back. All I knew was that I had to get the book and photo back to all of you. But by the time I got here, I guess I—"

"Collapsed." Dan frowned, pointing an accusatory beer at Alex. "Right in my arms as I opened the door. Like a baby."

Alex shook his head. Of course Dan had to give him crap right in front of Madison.

"I nursed him back to health like Florence-fucking-Nightingale." Dan seemed to be enjoying slipping into gunny sergeant mode, savoring every minute of slinging shit at Alex. Because billionaire or not, in front of Dan's little girl, Alex had no choice but to grin, eat it, and gush, "Mmm, what a chef."

"To set the record straight, I leaned on your shoulder. No one carried me like a baby," Alex said with a scowl, glancing at Madison, and she giggled at his *don't buy the hype* expression.

"Seriously, I wasn't sure what to make of him," Dan said. "He had Jack's book, and the photo, and apparently spent the last few months with Jack. Well, all that, and he probably had one hell of a story."

"Speaking of that," Alex said, suddenly remembering. "When's the last time you saw that photo?"

"Oh, I'm not sure. I mean, it should be in my office. Why?"

Madison leaned in. "Dad, a man gave me that photo and made up a pretty horrible story to go with it. We're trying to figure out how he got it. Alex explained that you gave him Jack's book, but that the photo should be here."

While Madison talked, Alex pulled up Frank Seaver's Google image on his phone, then handed it over to her.

Madison showed Dan. "This guy. Does he look familiar?"

"Oh, him." Dan shrugged at Alex. "The way he was poking around, I figured he was trying to get some dirt on you. The son of a bitch said you used this address, but that was nearly a decade ago, so anyone looking that far back had to be grasping at straws. I tried finding out what he was after, but I guess while I was busy fishing, he netted me. A few questions in, and he asked to use the bathroom. At the same time, I took a call. Telemarketer. Then he came out, thanked me, and left. Makes me wonder if anything else is missing."

Determined, Dan stood and headed into the house with

Madison and Alex on his heels. At the creak of the floors and the sunbeams hitting the sofa, Alex froze in midstep.

Maybe Madison had come and gone from here whenever she pleased, but not Alex. The last time he was here, he was barely holding on. Dan called it recovering. Like drawing a fine line between endlessly treading water and slowly drowning.

It hit him all at once.

The books on the bookshelf—he'd read them all. The quilt on the back of the sofa—which was his bed for the better part of a year. The photos on the walls—of the wife and daughter Alex always wondered about, but never prodded or asked. Even the smells—that same musty scent that would sit in his nose and hold him to the smallest shreds of life. Here and now.

His feelings were a mixture of sins and redemption, pain and hope. Alex needed a moment to take it all in, and Madison seemed to be giving it to him with a tight hug from behind, wrapping her arms around his waist and anchoring him to her.

"I'm right here," she said softly.

Alex sucked in a calming breath, easing his exhale and holding tight to her embrace. Somehow, just having her close chased away the ghosts of the past. He pulled her around and kissed her soft lips. "Thanks, beautiful. I needed that."

Dan returned in a huff, moving past them to the kitchen.

"What is it, Dad?"

"Nothing, maybe," he muttered. He opened a drawer, rummaging through it quietly, then shut it. Pensive, he returned to them. "He got the picture, but nothing else. Pisses me off that jackass got something off me."

Madison hugged Alex tighter, then looked up at him. "You might have something for Dad. In your wallet."

Smiling, Alex knew that look. Something in his wallet? No idea. But Madison had something up her sleeve, and Alex complied. Curious, he tugged the wallet from the back pocket of his jeans. Secured in the fold was the photo of him and Jack.

Before handing it over, he re-committed it to memory, ready to give it up to Dan. But Dan waved it away.

"You keep it. I've got another one." He motioned with his chin, pointing toward the bookshelf.

Quizzically, Madison and Alex both looked, not seeing what Dan meant. Then Alex noticed a frame that hadn't been there all those years ago.

Inside was a photo, trimmed with a solid black matting. It was the same as the one on Alex's baby grand piano—a picture of Madison and her dad smiling, holding up a photo. But this one was much bigger, at least twice the size of the one in Alex's place. And the photo of Madison and her dad? They were holding their own photo, and it was crystal clear. So clear, in fact, that Alex and Madison had to do a double-take.

What Madison and her dad were holding up all those years ago was the exact same photo Alex held now, with one unbelievable difference. It was completely intact, with a uniformed Staff Sergeant Paco Robles standing with his arm slung over Jack's shoulders, and Jack's arm tight around his waist. A beautiful snapshot frozen in time, magically recaptured into existence.

"Dad, how did you get this? How is this even possible?" Madison's words were fervent. Astonished. Holding an importance Alex wasn't sure he understood.

"Well, Jack called me from Italy. He wasn't supposed to, but he said he had something he needed to send me. Only . . ."

Alex felt something in his tone. "Only what?" Their trip to Italy was in the weeks before Jack was killed.

"Only, he said I wasn't supposed to have it. I'm guessing you all weren't supposed to have any evidence of your mission. In fact, he told me flat-out that after I saw it, I should print it but put it somewhere safe, and delete the digital copy. No record of the email could exist. Instead, I printed it out and grabbed Madison before she ran out with her friends. We took a quick shot of a picture within a picture. I emailed that back to him. I knew he'd get it, but no one else would understand. Hidden in plain sight. For us to share."

"This is incredible," Madison said softly, admiring it.

Dan pointed back to the bookshelf. "Just like the one I printed for you, Alex. Except I wanted yours to be small enough that you could keep it in your wallet, since neither of us were exactly sure where you'd land after you left."

Madison swooped over and picked up the frame like a precious gift. Her eyes gleamed as she held it reverently in her hands, murmuring, "Hidden in plain sight."

Alex noticed a tear rolling down her cheek and brushed it away with his thumb. "What is it?"

Laughing through her tears, she looked first at Alex, then at her dad. "It's us," she said, then explained. "It's all of us. Our family."

CHAPTER 26

MADISON

Up well before the crack of dawn, Madison looked over at Alex. Waking up before the workaholic mogul gave her a small thrill, and she watched him slumber away. His breathing was deep and restful, as if for the first time ever, he could relax.

Let's keep it that way.

The sound of rustling elsewhere in the house meant the old gunnery sergeant was up and at 'em. Sliding from the curve of Alex's strong arm, she slipped from the bed and out of the room, following the light to the kitchen.

"Coffee, jellybean?" Dan asked with his back to her.

In her warm socks, Madison skated across the kitchen floor and wrapped a warm hug around him. "No sneak attack on you. Coffee sounds great."

Dan handed her a cup as she scrounged through the fridge for anything that would pass as cream. A small carton of two-percent was close enough to its expiration date that it would do. Sugar was permanently planted front and center on the table, with a small stack of pennies for company.

"So, you and AJ," Dan said. "What's going on there?"

Her father wasn't looking at her, but took his seat and

patiently waited, stirring a few spoons of sugar into the instant brew. Satisfied with his usual amount of sweetness, he put the spoon down and took the mug in his hands, cupping it close but not taking a sip. He just studied the ripples across the surface as he blew, then watched her through the escaping steam.

Madison sat down next to him and scooted her chair close, grabbing his spoon and helping herself to the sugar. "Something, I don't know . . . wonderful." The chance of concealing from her father how head over heels she was for Alex was definitely zero.

With a deep whiff of the coffee that always reminded her of home, she took a long, slow sip and waited for her dad's reaction.

But Dan didn't react, simply resumed his Maxwell House stare-down over the rim of his cup. Her cheesy smile must have been too much. "Does he make you happy? Take care of you?"

His parental squint was unmistakable. Truth serum in a stare. She might as well be ten years old again.

Madison set down her cup to clasp his hands. They were tight around his mug, almost white-knuckled with worry. "Dad, I'm happier than I've ever been in my life. He really does take care of me, and I hope he feels like I take care of him too."

Knowing she was positively glowing, she enjoyed being able to share something wonderful with her dad. Pleased, she released his hands and took another sip.

"Well, you've both been through a lot." He took a gulp and let out a small laugh. "Between the two of you, I couldn't tell you who I've worried about more."

"Hmm, your fiercely independent, introverted, occasional basket case of a daughter falls for a high-profile and intermittently tortured workaholic. I take it you're not worried now, are you?" Her grin ticked up with an air of whimsy.

Sitting back, he relaxed. "Nope, not worried at all. But I guess it's time I let you in on a little secret."

More Alex secrets? I. Am. Listening.

"Remember when I asked you if you if you needed money for

anything? Getting settled? Giving college a try? Or if you needed anything before you went to New York?"

Madison nodded.

"But you," he said, reaching out to tap the tip of her nose, "*you* always said no. Why?"

Why? It was Madison's turn to stare down the dark liquid steaming in her cup. "I don't know. I guess I just really wanted to make it on my own. You made your own way, and so did Jack."

"Jack had a scholarship."

"Jack *earned* his scholarship. He was so excited starting his career. I knew it was because he did it all on his own. I wanted that, something I earned all on my own. Because with you, and Jack, and even Mom with her real estate, why should I be any different?" Madison shrugged. "After what happened to Jack, I just felt like exploring my options. Trying new things. Checking out the world. And I loved every job, every journey, and every life-long friend I've made along the way. I'm not sure I'd be the same person without them, and I wouldn't change a thing."

Dan raised a brow at her. "So, you don't regret not taking me up on the money?"

The money. Like there was any. Madison's dad would have given up anything and everything he had for her. Knowing that was enough. It pushed her to work harder than anyone around her so she would never have to ask him for a dime.

"Nope. No regrets."

Dan gave her a big grin. "Why don't you take a look in that drawer over there."

"The junk drawer?"

Sure. Maybe there's a new stash of pens, paper clips, or rubber bands.

Madison opened the first drawer. On top was a *TV Guide* from 1985. "Charlie's Angels?" she asked, holding it up.

Dan scoffed. "Not that drawer. The next one."

The next one was a mystery, filled with letter upon letter. A hundred of them, maybe more. All were addressed to Dan Taylor in a familiar handwriting with sweeping strokes and the smallest tail on the n's.

Alex.

Her fingers walked across the top of them, checking out a few for the date they were postmarked. They went back years. The return addresses varied, but they were all from the same person. *AJ Drake.* As far as she could tell, none had been opened. She grabbed the top handful and turned back to Dan.

"Dad, what is all this?"

Dan looked over. "Jellybean, that was AJ's personal trust fund for you. Well, and me, I guess. He sent these a few times a year. I stopped opening them when they stopped including letters, just checks. But I never cashed one. I *did* keep them, though. as a reminder of AJ."

Madison couldn't help but hold one of the more recent ones up to the light. Then another. And another.

"Dad! This is some serious money."

"Yes, Frankie, it is. But AJ earned it, not me, and I didn't need it. I thought maybe someday you would. Checks are only good for six months, I guess, because he kept upping the amount. Like a running tally. Some crazy, personal lotto, right? I figured I'd have them just in case you ever needed them."

She took a second, then plopped back down on the chair next to Dan, staring in total disbelief at a handful of envelopes that had to contain the equivalent of the net worth of a few countries.

Dan snagged one and waved it in front of her face. "I just needed to let you know. Without knowing you or asking for a single thing in return, AJ's been trying to take care of you since way before now. And I guess a small part of me is glad he finally gets the chance."

Madison looked down at the envelopes fanned out in her hands, thinking of Alex as he lay blissfully asleep. Urgently, she checked the time. "Dad, I need to go out for a while. Can you keep Alex occupied?"

"Good old-fashioned diversionary mission?" He picked up a penny from a small pile on the table and slid it to Madison. "I'm all in."

Madison swiped the penny, palming it tight as she headed over for a rushed hug. "Thanks, Dad."

Grabbing her bag, she slipped out into the dark morning.

CHAPTER 27

ALEX

Alex's deep sleep was interrupted by a loud crack and rumble, the distinct rev of the Big Banana, Paco's—*no, Madison's*—yellow Lamborghini.

"Madison?" he mumbled, grogginess clouding his vision as he looked around. He stretched himself awake. Rolling over, he slid a hand over the sheet on her side of the bed. Cool to the touch. The lightweight blanket wouldn't hold the heat in, though, so maybe she hadn't been gone long.

Slipping on a pair of sweats and a T-shirt, he headed out of the room and followed the light emerging from the rustic kitchen. Madison's father was busy fixing a cup of coffee, though there were two on the table.

"Black, right?" Dan asked.

"Right," Alex said with a yawn. He accepted the fresh cup gratefully and sat in a seat that was definitely warm beneath his butt.

Curious, he slipped a hand around what had to be Madison's mug, still half-full. The warmth remained. Dan pursed his lips in amusement, and Alex could feel his scrutiny.

"Well?" Dan said, beginning the test. "What can you tell me?"

Sipping from his own mug, Alex's free hand held Madison's abandoned cup for a moment. "She's been gone a few minutes, which only confirms what I already knew, since she opted to blow out of suburbia revving at a hundred thirty decibels. But, from how Madison indulges in coffee, she must have had a bit of a heart-to-heart with dear old Dad."

Dan smirked, and Alex continued.

"Her cup's warm enough that, even with the ambient coolness of the room, I'd say you two were talking for twenty, maybe twenty-five minutes at the most. On top of which, she decided to leave suddenly. Not a lot of pre-thought. Otherwise, she would have paced herself to either finish her coffee faster, or just pass on it altogether."

He glanced up at Dan, who nodded.

"I love my little girl, but a covert escape in the dark of morning is just not her style," Dan said, and they both chuckled. "Madison had to go do something, but she'll be back a little later."

A sip of the piping-hot coffee warmed Alex from the inside out, the flavor pulling him back to so many mornings past, long ago. Funny how the inexpensive brew always managed to ease him. "You know, I forgot how great your coffee is."

"Good to the last fucking drop." Dan held up his mug in a toast, then drained the last of it before standing again to get a refill. Once he'd poured himself another cup, he lingered at the counter. "AJ, can I ask you something?"

"Anything."

"Do you still have my phone number buried somewhere in that highfalutin phone of yours? Maybe not in the top ten, but somewhere?"

Alex said quickly, "Well, you were number one, but got bumped about three and a half weeks ago."

"That's interesting. See, Frankie and I caught up a little, and it all strikes me as, well, odd. Why didn't you just call me and ask for her number?"

"Because that would have been too easy. And you know me, Dan. It's the hard way or no way."

"Seriously?"

"Seriously." Alex let his head fall back before raking his fingers through his hair. With a long sigh, he sat up straight again. "I guess I didn't feel right about it, with how much you'd helped me. Everything you did for me. I think it would have been, I don't know, rude maybe. Like, *hey, thanks for saving me from myself and all, letting me crash at your place for months on end, and nursing me back from the brink of death. By the way, I'd like a go at your daughter. What's her number?*"

Dan smirked. "Well, good to see that at the very least, you're still so goddamned polite. But with your resources, you could have had her information in a New York minute."

Perplexed with himself, Alex shook his head. "If I couldn't ask you to your face, I sure as hell wasn't going to do surveillance behind your back, no matter how trivial it seemed." He pushed out a long breath. "I wasn't sure I'd be good for anyone, let alone *your* daughter and *Jack's* little sister. And meeting Madison wasn't exactly premeditated. I mean, I didn't set out to do it."

After taking another sip of his coffee, he pushed on. "But I don't know, I couldn't shake this feeling. I just kept getting the sense that we were going to meet, run into each other, almost as if—"

"As if by fate?" It was Dan's turn to be perplexed and shake his head. "Damn, son, are you telling me that under all that hard-charging exterior bullshit, you're a hopeless fucking romantic?"

Alex smiled at the teasing before explaining further.

"The first time I saw her, it was only a hunch. I didn't actually know who she was until after our first, um . . ." He glanced nervously at Dan, careful as he continued. "Our first date. Not fate, exactly, but I don't know, like maybe someone was looking down on us. Lending a hand."

Dan scowled at him. "Jack wouldn't lend you a hand." Then

his glare melted into a broad grin. "Jack's style would've been a swift kick in the ass."

Alex laughed out a relieved breath.

"Well, be it fate or friendly forces," Dan said, "I can't think of two people better suited for each other. And I know you'd tear out your own heart before you'd break Frankie's."

"I would." Alex beamed at Dan, grateful for another round of fatherly bonding with him. It had been so long. Too long. But here Dan was, once again appearing in Alex's life at just the right time, being the father he'd never had.

Dawn was breaking in the distance, and a ray of sunlight pierced through the kitchen window, striking a row of pennies along its ledge.

Alex's gaze followed the beam to the table, sparkling against the small copper pile in the center of it. "You know, I forgot about all the pennies around here. They're in Madison's room too."

Grabbing one off the windowsill, Dan tossed it to him.

Catching it easily, Alex smiled as he admired it for a second. "You threw one at me when I left. I guess they're pretty lucky."

"These pennies aren't about luck. They're about loyalty. Risk. Never giving up. Don't you know the saying *in for a penny?*"

Alex downed another sip. "Something like *in for a penny, in for a pound?*"

Dan nodded.

"Okay. So, what does it mean?"

"Back in the day, the Brits coined it, saying if hanging was the punishment regardless of the crime, why not go for broke? If I stole a penny, and it had the same punishment as a larger crime, I might as well steal a pound. But we red-blooded Americans took it to the next level. If I'm gonna risk anything, I might as well risk everything. If I'm going to start something, I'm gonna see it through to the end. In our family, we always used it to show we had each other's back, through thick and thin."

Alex thought of the penny Madison had left on his desk. There was so much meaning behind it, and after just one night together.

Could I love Madison Taylor more?

"That you?" Dan asked, interrupting Alex's faraway stare to alert him to the faint ring of his cell from the bedroom.

He hurried back, picking it up a second too late. It was Gina's office line. And at 6:40 in the morning, it had to be important. Before he could dial back, her devil-horned avatar displayed again. This time, he was quick to accept.

"Hey, Gina. You're up early."

"Not my idea, I assure you. But that's what happens when I hear a competitor's VP is coming in for a meeting."

"It has to be a mistake. I don't have anything on my calendar. Did you check with Paco?"

"That's just it. He's not answering, and Madison Taylor seems to be assigned to meet with the VP. It's an invite from your calendar."

What? "With who?"

"That d-bag Frank Seaver. Are you okay with this?"

Hell no, I'm not okay with this. Madison said she didn't know how that son of a bitch got the contract. And yet here she is meeting with him. While I'm all of a sudden out of town.

"Boss?"

Alex settled down, not wanting to bring Gina into the angst of his love life. As the head of human capital for DGI, plausible deniability was her preferred default. "Yes, I guess I am. Do me a favor. Send me the details, but don't let anyone know I know." Two seconds later, a text pinged his phone with the time and location of the meeting. "Got it."

"Do you need me to get a car to you?"

Calculating the distance, he declined. "There's no time for that." He looked out Madison's bedroom window, noting an open field next to the house. "But I've got a faster ride. Thanks, Gina."

He hung up, sent a quick text, then scrolled to number five in his favorites. He clicked it, and after a few rings, the call was picked up.

"Hey, man," Alex said. "I'm gonna need to call in that favor. I just texted you my location, and bring the baby."

"Everything all right?" Dan was at his door, handing Alex a fresh cup.

With his thumb disconnecting the call, Alex painted on a smile. "Fine. Work stuff," he said, not wanting to involve Dan. Or worry him.

Dan scowled at him. "You really think you can clam up on me and think I won't see right through it?"

"Nope." Alex huffed out a resigned sigh. "You're right. It's just . . ."

Hesitating, he considered what actually weighed on his mind, and what he should share with Dan. The fact that Madison headed back to the city without him? Setting up a meeting from his calendar? Taking a meeting with one of the scuzziest people on the planet without a word to him?

I guess when she said, "I'm not going anywhere," she meant for the night.

Dan didn't need to know all that, so Alex tossed out an obvious comment, sharing his observations but not sounding overly concerned.

"It's just that it doesn't seem like Madison to leave half a cup of coffee behind." He smiled, only half joking about the girl who could nurse a cappuccino for hours.

"No, it doesn't. I'm sure she'll be back soon."

"I wouldn't bet on it." Alex let out a slow, uncertain breath. Dan deserved the truth. Or some of it, at least. "Your little girl's hightailing it back to Manhattan."

"What?" Agitated, Dan flailed his hands, nearly sloshing his coffee beyond the rim. "I've got four pounds of short ribs marinating. I was counting on Frankie to tackle at least a pound of them."

"Well, if she doesn't, I'll eat every last rib because they're amazing. But don't worry. I'm heading that way now. Come hell or high water, I'll be back. With Madison. And a real New York cheesecake."

Alex's adamance must have been apparent because Dan smirked, relaxing with another sip. "Sounds like my little girl's giving you a run for your money."

God, I hope not.

CHAPTER 28

ALEX

Once the helicopter came in for a soft landing in the open field, Alex hurried over and hopped in, waving back to Dan.

Dan called out, and Alex could read his lips. *Don't forget the cheesecake.*

He returned a solid thumbs-up, hoping like hell he could keep the other half of his commitment to Dan. He slipped on the waiting headset and fastened himself in, speaking into the mic. "I owe you, man."

Mark toggled several switches and gave him an annoying grin. "Well, I do like it when Alex Drake owes me. I've had my eye on a yacht..."

Running through the lines of the memorized checklist, Alex received clearance from the nearest tower, took over as pilot, and they were off. By the unsteady climb, Alex could see his emotions were a little volatile. Mark noticed too, of course, and placed a steady hand on his own cyclic.

"Easy, partner," Mark said. "Maybe it's been a hot second since you've handled this pristine piece of machinery, but trust me, she likes a gentle touch."

"She?" Alex asked. "Sounds like you and she are getting close."

"Her name is Lola, and yes, we are."

Mark motioned to take back control. Figuring it was in their best interest to arrive as fast as possible but in one piece, Alex gratefully acquiesced.

"Want to take a load off?" Mark asked. "My psychotherapy rates are pretty reasonable."

Alex scoffed. "Liar. You'd take me for every penny I have . . . and Lola too."

"True," Mark said without bothering to argue the point. "Let's begin your session. Should we open with some deep-breathing exercises? I hear Lamaze can get you in a nice, relaxed state."

Alex rolled his eyes, not joining in on Mark's laughter.

For kicks, Mark hung a hard left, taking them down with enough of a drop to feel like a roller coaster. For the first time in an hour, Alex smiled. A genuine smile.

When Mark came to the authorized altitude, he eased into a fast but comfortable speed. "So, what's on your mind?"

"You know your old pal Seaver?"

"Yeah . . ." Mark gave him a wary glance. "Come on, Alex. You don't need to snarl every time you say his name. Frank might be a bastard, but he's damn good at his job."

"Madison is meeting with him. In two and a half hours."

Mark whipped his head around. "Why the fuck is she doing that?"

And there it was. Mark knew it too. There would be no reason for a junior analyst to be meeting with the *damn good at his job* ass-wipe.

"Who knows? All I know is she did it on a whim. Didn't let me know. Didn't let her father know. She headed back to the city without a word. Speaking of her father, you'll be eating with us tonight at his house. We're having ribs."

"You don't have to twist my arm. But don't veer from the subject at hand. Back to Madison."

Uncertain how to inch into the shallow end of a topic that

instantly dropped a thousand feet deep, Alex started with an unsettled shrug. "Maybe with Madison, I jumped the gun on our relationship—"

"You?" Mark's feigned look of surprise was met with Alex's glare. "And define *relationship*," he said, stretching out the word for effect. "Are we even at ten weeks yet?"

"As a matter of fact, we are." *If we count from the very first time we met.* "So, go fuck yourself. Anyway, as I was saying and to your point, maybe I need to . . . I don't know . . . back off and let it evolve naturally. Build something based on trust."

"Or lust," Mark said, waggling his brows. "It comes a close second. And it rhymes."

Mark was enjoying this way too much. It was the first time Alex had come anywhere near a serious talk about his first real relationship. Waist deep in uncharted territory, he was grateful for the ear of a man happily married to the love of his life. Ready to receive every bit of wisdom, sarcasm, and judgment this man had, Alex pressed on.

"The thing is, I . . . I have no fucking idea what to do. I'm going out of my goddamn mind wondering what the hell is going on. And . . ." He sucked in a breath, barely able to admit this to himself, let alone to the man he considered a brother. "I might have handed her the keys to my kingdom on nothing more than blind faith."

"What do you mean?" Mark gave him a sharp look.

Alex stared at the view a moment before continuing. "I might have given her full access to my calendar."

"So? Everyone in your inner circle has that. Jess and I have it too."

"Well, she set up the meeting with Seaver by sending him an invitation . . . from my calendar. So now it looks like I've made a meeting with him. On top of which, he apparently had access to private information."

"Information? Like, the sort of information that puts you in a compromising position? Tell me it's not more than your occasional indulgence in chick flicks and romance novels?"

"More like a commitment I made to Madison. In private. I wanted her to get to know me better, and basically swore I'd never lie to her."

"And that's a risk because..."

"Because I said that if I ever lied to her . . . and the operative word is *if* . . . she'd be entitled to all my corporate and personal assets."

With a deep chuckle, Mark marveled at his friend. "Wow. Way to make the rest of us look like underachievers. I wouldn't worry about it, though. It's not like you lied. Or put in in writing."

Clearing his throat and rubbing a newly formed ache at his temple, Alex said slowly, "I might have put it in writing. And had Paco witness it."

The somber look on Mark's face reflected every pang of torment Alex was already feeling.

"Oh, it gets worse. According to Madison, she has no idea how he got a hold of it, but it was in her possession. At the penthouse. It's not like she dropped it on the way to work. Seaver is an attorney. He knows what he's got. Maybe they're in it together."

The silence was stifling. Mark didn't say a word, but rather sat quietly, processing it, no doubt mentally pelting Alex with an imaginative assortment of colorful names.

Eventually, Mark made eye contact, looking Alex up and down until a high degree of certainty filled his face. "Well, well, well. Sounds like Alex Drake is in love." Which was immediately followed by Mark singing, "Alex has Madison sitting on his tree . . ."

Alex huffed out a frustrated breath. "I'm serious. What if I was wrong about us? About her? Trusted her when maybe I shouldn't have. And for reasons I don't want to talk about, maybe there's a part of her that can never forgive me for my past. Whether she's calculating and conniving, or just young and naive, it doesn't matter. Either way, I'm fucked. Paco was right. I put not just me, but my whole goddamned corporation at risk. Globally, thousands of jobs. Not to mention everything I owe to the shareholders. It was irresponsible."

"It was decisive."

Frowning, Alex shook his head. "I need to take a step back. Slow down. Maybe put things on pause, at least for the moment. Think more. Feel less."

Mark took an aggressive and dangerous nosedive before pulling up. Gripping a hand strap, Alex forgot the luxury chopper was built for maneuverability as well as speed until Mark's little trick reminded him. Apparently, his friend seemed intent on getting his attention before laying into him.

"I'm not sure at what point you turned eighty-five," Mark said fiercely, "but it looks like shit on you, man. You made billions by shooting from the hip, using the fucking Force, and trusting your gut. And now, because you're not the one in control, you run? Is that what you want? A life that's safe and secure? Empty as fuck and boring as shit? Because I doubt it, and I'm pretty sure those aren't the qualities that drew Madison to you in the first place. And isn't it part of Madison's allure that you can't control the woman? News flash. Women can't be controlled. The sooner you come to grips with that, the better."

Crossing his arms over his chest, Alex didn't respond, pressing his lips into a tight line as he contemplated Mark's words for the next fifteen minutes of their ride. Silently, he lined up a few plays in his head, finally deciding on the best course of action.

It must have been written all over his face, because when Mark glanced at him again, his face broke into a huge grin. "Well? What are we doing? And who's going with you?"

"Going with me?" Alex met Mark's grin with a devious smile. "Oh, I think you and I both know who I'm bringing."

"I had a hunch."

Alex gave them both a critical once-over, running a hand over his own grown-out scruff and taking in how Mark had graduated from burly lumberjack to potential cast member of *Duck Dynasty*. "Well, first things first. Barber, then tailor. There's zero chance I'm barging into a meeting looking like this, and frankly, you could use a makeover."

Mark checked the clock. "Do we have enough time?"

"Trust me, Rip Van Winkle, we're making time."

CHAPTER 29

MADISON

Madison decided to wear her most serious black-on-black suit, conveying both the gravity of the situation as well as armoring up for what could be one hell of a fight. Though Paco had insisted on joining her, she'd adamantly declined. This was her fight. She'd do it alone.

On her way to DGI's conference room 214, she calmed her nerves by thinking of Alex. He'd walked her through those crazy self-defense moves after rescuing her from the street thugs, patient with her until she nailed each one. The powerful mogul had taken his valuable time to give her a one-on-one self-defense lesson, imparting a few words of advice to make her safer. Stronger. And in the face of danger, a more worthy opponent.

Here goes nothing.

Arriving in the conference room a few minutes early, she took the seat at the head of the table. The power seat. And the perfect vantage point to take in all of Frank Seaver as he strutted through the door a moment later.

"My dear, you look ravishing. So well suited at the head of the table. Exactly where the CEO should be." He strolled up to greet her, leaning over as if to give her a kiss on the cheek.

Because his balls are definitely bigger than his brains.

Madison leaned back, extending a firm arm and insisting on the professionalism of a faraway handshake. Nothing says *back the fuck up* like a stiff arm and a glare.

Seaver smiled, then kissed her hand. The slobbery lip print he left made her wince.

Gross. She pulled her hand back, wiping it on the chair and making a mental note to return with a gallon bottle of bleach.

"Now, my dear, is that any way to treat the man you're getting into bed with?"

Madison managed to swallow the bile rising in her throat. "Oh, I'm not getting into bed with you, Mr. Seaver. Figuratively or otherwise."

Dismissively, she waved her hand, giving him permission to sit. Once he did, she clasped her hands on the conference table, powering up for her play.

"I'm here to tell you that you don't have a deal, and you don't have my vote. I'm sorry you've wasted your time, but there's nothing left for you."

"If that's your position, very well." His words were too easy, and she watched him relax back in his seat. "Let me ask you something, Ms. Taylor. Is it difficult? Living with the guilt."

"What guilt?" *He's baiting me. He has to be.*

"Oh, the guilt that your brother sold out his country for a few measly dollars."

"That's a goddamned lie!" Madison's rage got the better of her before she could reel it in. But tears would be so much worse. She had to bite the inside of her cheek to keep from crying.

How dare he disparage Jack that way?

"Maybe," Seaver said smugly, "but I've got friends that tell me otherwise. Like, that his treason was covered up. Or maybe they'll just say what I want them to say. Who needs proof when there's social media, and a senator or two in your pocket? Wow, I might be sitting on the exposé of the year."

"What do you want?" Madison demanded impatiently, now thoroughly irate. "I told you, I don't have any shares for any proxy vote."

"You don't now, but you will." With a smarmy smile, he took out a contract, placing it before her along with a pen. "I'm going to make this so easy for you. All you have to do is sign. That's it. No muss, no fuss. Just a signature away from being a world-class millionaire."

Confused, Madison took a moment to scan the contract, pretty sure he'd ignored everything she'd said. "This says I'm signing over all my shares to you," she said as she tossed it onto the table. "Shares I don't have."

"It doesn't matter. Between your contract with Drake"— Seaver pulled out the original taped-together contract Alex had given her and laid it next to the contract she'd just thrown down —"and mine with you, it's all I'll need."

"Aren't you forgetting something? Alex Drake would have had to lie to me for his contract with me to be valid. He's never lied. Not once."

Seaver leaned back in his chair with a chuckle. "He doesn't have to. With your signature on that piece of paper, a lie is implied. It's all I need, enough to force him out. Drake will be left with two choices—a scandal or a buyout. My bet's on the buyout. Oh, and your brother can rest in peace. See? One little signature, and it's win, win, win." He nudged the Mont Blanc pen closer to her. "Now, wouldn't you like an ending where everybody wins?"

Madison considered the sleazebag's offer. She thought of what Jack would have wanted. And her father. Then there was Paco, and all the sacrifices he'd already made for Jack.

Finally, she thought of Alex, and his words came back to her. He wanted peace and freedom, and her. He was ready for an exit strategy, ready to take whatever golden parachute buyout was offered and run with it.

Her arm itched like a son of a bitch, but the hives would have to wait.

Glaring at Seaver, she took the pen and held it up. "Mr. Seaver, why don't you shove this pen right up your ass? No matter what you threaten me with, I'm not signing. Do what you will."

Tossing the pen on the table, Madison stood, prepared to leave. But when the door to the conference room opened before she left the table, her jaw dropped.

CHAPTER 30

MADISON

"You kids trying to have a meeting without us?" Alex asked as Madison stared in awe. Alex was bright-eyed with the confidence of a man who'd spent years accustomed to having the upper hand.

"They grow up so darn fast," his companion said, a man sporting an equally impressive suit and demeanor.

Alarmed, Seaver jumped to his feet. "Mr. Donovan, what are you doing here?"

Madison recognized the name, but not the man. Mr. Donovan, also known as *the Sniper*. The hard-charging CEO of Excelsior/Centurion, Frank Seaver's boss, and Alex Drake's most aggressive competitor.

"*Now* the meeting can begin," Donovan said as he and Alex crossed the room.

They made their way to the conference table, but the Sniper went out of his way to walk over to Madison. Rattled, she stepped back from her chair, ready to relinquish her seat to either of the two high-powered CEOs.

He shook her hand, then firmly nudged her back to her seat. She realized as she lowered herself into it that he was slipping something into the palm of her hand. "It's good to see you again, Ms. Taylor."

See me again?

Madison's reaction volleyed between skepticism and irritation . . . at herself. First, she couldn't recall meeting Alex, and now this Manhattan CEO had apparently been met and forgotten too.

Really? her inner voice wailed. *Another one?*

As the gentlemen—and Slimy Seaver—took their seats, she held her hands in her lap, then looked down in bewilderment when she opened her hand. Donovan had given her a shiny new penny. Staring at him, she leaned back in her chair, uncertain where any of this was going.

Eyeing Seaver, Mr. Donovan spoke harshly. "Are we resorting to strong-arming analysts now to force a competitive edge? It's not exactly what we're known for."

Blinking rapidly, Seaver remained silent.

From his blazer pocket, Mr. Donovan retrieved a pair of glasses, slipped them on, then scooped up the contracts on the table. He held them up high to read them, hiding his face from Seaver, but allowing him to privately grace Madison with the assurance of two long wink-winks.

His smile was infectious. And familiar.

Abruptly, he snapped the pages with annoyance and handed them to Alex. With his glasses on, Madison finally realized who he was and gasped.

Add a shaggy beard and a layer of easygoing flannel and he was Jess's husband, Mark, aka "Mr. Bishop." Or, as he was often referred to in headlines in the *New York Times*, *Marcus* Donovan.

"That sheet of paper's in pretty rough shape," Mark said. "And here I thought your days of dumpster diving were over."

Seaver admitted nothing while Alex reviewed the tattered document, admiring his own work.

"This little baby is well-written, concise, and fairly generous of me. But if someone were thinking of using it, and I'm not being overly critical, there's just one little hiccup. You see, despite the arts-and-crafts way it's been taped back together, it was obviously torn up, crumpled, and discarded. Meaning that the owner at the time, indicated here to be one Ms. Madison Taylor, didn't seem to want it."

Mark raised a brow at his employee. "Seaver, you're slipping. You're an attorney. Don't they teach you anything at law school? To be a binding contract, there are several elements that must be met. The first is offer. And the second is?"

Shifting in his seat, Seaver averted his gaze as he mumbled, "Acceptance."

Mixing his arrogance with fun, Mark rejoiced. "Yes, Seaver, *acceptance*. I knew you'd get there if we dropped enough bread crumbs for you. And a contract that was torn up, crumpled, and discarded seems proof positive that there was no actual *acceptance*. But let's just verify that, shall we? Ms. Taylor, do you accept the terms of this contract?"

All eyes turned to Madison.

She sat up, gripping the penny a little harder as she directed her stern words at Seaver. "No, I don't."

Mark clapped a hand on Seaver's shoulder, grabbing his attention. "There. No acceptance. The contract is not binding. Ms. Taylor is not the owner of any of the shares of DGI." Puzzled, he exchanged a glance with Alex. "But you know what's really bothering me, Mr. Drake?"

"What's that, Mr. Donovan?"

"It's the odd way that Seaver, my senior VP, went about this. Hiding his intentions from me, his boss, the CEO of Excelsior/Centurion. Hmm, makes one wonder."

Alex smirked. "Indeed, it does."

"I'm guessing," Mark said, "it's because this little scheme wasn't about DGI at all. Well, it was a little about DGI, but it was really about E/C. The hostile takeover of your company paved the path to a different scheme. This wasn't about giving E/C the proxy vote, but to giving *Seaver* the proxy. So, why stop there? He would have a license to hunt. If he did that, a merger between DGI and E/C would be imminent, and the next step in Seaver's plan at world domination? I suspect it would be my own golden parachute."

Alex chimed in. "And, no doubt, a less than generous one at that." He gave Mark a consoling pat on the back.

Seaver jumped to his feet. "Mr. Donovan, this is a complete misunderstanding. You can't possibly doubt my loyalty to you."

A deadly smile ticked up Mark's lips. "Seaver, if there's one thing I know, it's that the only loyalty you've got is to yourself. Lucky for me, you've violated several terms of your employment, including misrepresenting the interests of E/C and me. So, with that, I'm pleased to inform you that you are no longer employed by or represent Excelsior/Centurion. At all."

Seaver huffed out, "You can't fire me. I'm on the board of directors."

Alex grinned. "Well, I'm sure they'd love to see how you really operate." He pointed to a corner of the ceiling, where a camera stared down at them. "Smile pretty." Dropping the pretense of cordiality, he gave Seaver a lethal glare that would cower most men. "Let me break it down for you. If anything is leaked to smear any of us, or anyone in Ms. Taylor's family, that little footage is going be the viral video of the year."

Mark pulled a folded piece of paper from his breast pocket and handed it to Seaver. "Now, *I'm* gonna make this easy for *you*. Sign this resignation, and your ass stays out of jail."

The blood drained from Seaver's face, and his hand shook a little as he reached for the pen. Marcus Donovan was infamous for his threats, and just as well known for always backing them up. Seaver steadied his hand, quickly signed, then raced out of the room without another word.

Alex and Mark snickered, amused and pleased as they

watched him leave. With him out of the way, they both turned their attention to Madison.

"You okay?" Alex asked.

"I—I think so," she said before turning to Mark. "So, you're Marcus Donovan. CEO of Excelsior/Centurion. The biggest rival of DGI. The Wall Street *Sniper*. Yet, you two are best friends?"

Mark patted her hand. "Well, yes. And yes. Alex and I built our companies, and our friendships, around the same time. We both knew that to get an edge and keep it, we needed to stay sharp. We couldn't do that by coddling each other. We needed to compete. Hard. So, we've kept our friendship low-key, but have always championed each other behind the scenes."

Alex interjected. "It's the same with martial arts. I can't get better if people *let* me win. I have to earn it. Keep pushing, and learning, and growing. Otherwise, my skills atrophy until I'm defenseless. Our fierce competitive streak keeps us on our toes, and ensures our respective companies are always the best of the best."

As Madison listened, it was easy to see why they were close, and how they managed to make it all work without anyone knowing. What wasn't easy to see was how they got to the meeting in time. "I seriously hauled butt to get to the city, change clothes, and prepare for battle. I can't believe you got here so fast."

Pinning her with his dark gaze, Alex leaned closer from across the table. "And I can't believe you tore up that contract."

Despite the heat rising between the two of them, the savage hunger in his eyes and the wetness between her legs, they weren't exactly alone.

Deliberately, Mark cleared his throat to remind them. "It's a piece of cake when I'm the custodian of Alex's sexy new baby, which cruises at a comfortable one hundred seventy-five miles per hour."

Her furrowed brow relaxed, but the wheels in her head still

spun like crazy. "And the camera? I was just in this room a few days ago. Conference room 214 doesn't have cameras. Everyone knows it."

Alex weighed in with a broad, boyish grin. "You're right. Everyone knows there's no cameras in this conference room, including Seaver. When I discovered the meeting, I had a small crew install the equipment. Life's good when you're the head of a company renowned for surveillance." He took Madison's closed hand. "You sure you're okay?"

The penny was warm in her palm. Relieved, she smiled at them both, letting out a long breath with her response. "I am now."

Alex stood and pulled her to her feet, wrapping her in a warm embrace. "And for the record, the terms of the contract were never satisfied. I'm sorry, Ms. Taylor, but under the circumstances, there's no way you could get all my assets."

Alarmed, she opened her mouth to protest, but her argument was stopped by his finger against her lips.

"I'm afraid the most I could possibly give you is, well . . . half. And maybe a shredder for Christmas."

Madison's eyes widened, but Alex gave her no chance to respond as he stole a series of soft, warm kisses.

CHAPTER 31

MADISON

A week later

The ballroom was alive with music and chatter as Madison and her escort made their way into the reception. Crossing the grand ballroom, she floated past the head table, wearing a gown that luminously trailed her every move. The silvery lace was enhanced with jet-black accents, its elegance perfect for a magical night.

Taking her seat at another table, she practically beamed, an odd contrast to her sulking escort who dropped into the chair next to her. Drumming his fingers on the table, Paco seemed thoroughly annoyed.

"Oh, *hermanita*," he said, seething with suspicion.

"Yes, brother dear?" Madison coyly replied.

His pursed lips unlocked to vent. "I might be okay with bringing you here because, as you said, the RSVP was already sent and the seats were already assigned. *And* I might even be okay with you not taking your proper seat at the head table to hang out with me here, because you're an angel and that's just the person you are. But I'm not—let me repeat—*not* okay with the two of us stuck all alone at a table for five."

Snatching up an elegant place card from the table, he fumed. "Other than yours and mine, the place cards aren't even filled in. *VIP Guest.* What the hell is a VIP guest? We'd both better damn well be VIP guests, but at least we have names. This is too high school for words. What the hell is going on?"

Madison shrugged, bringing a glass of bubbly at her lips to avoid answering. As she sipped, she caught a glimpse of one of the very, very VIPs in question, and waved him over with glee.

Paco turned, checking out the person Madison was summoning. Noticeably shocked, Paco stood and chugged his full glass of champagne, then reached for hers and downed it as well. "You didn't say your father was coming."

"I didn't? Oh. Well, he's coming." She nudged the bottle of Moët just out of reach. As Paco tried reaching for the bottle to pour himself another glass of courage, she whispered, "Don't be nervous. He hardly ever makes anyone drop and give him twenty anymore."

Madison stood and threw herself into her father's arms for a tight squeeze. "Dad, I'm so glad you could make it. You look amazing."

Dan beamed at her. "Well, AJ hooked me up with this monkey suit, and wearing it to mow the lawn or work on the car seemed a bit much."

Paco couldn't sneak back a few steps without Madison grabbing his arm and yanking him near.

"Dad, I want you to meet someone very special." Madison pushed Paco's hesitant body right in front of her dad. "This," she said ceremoniously, "is Paco. Paco, this is my dad, Dan."

Madison watched Paco snap to attention, as if Gunnery Sergeant Dan were in uniform and on duty.

With Paco nervous and Dan impatient, Madison second-guessed the brilliance of her idea. The lights lowered, and the DJ transitioned the music to a ballad.

Surprising Madison, Dan barked out an assertive demand. "Let's dance."

Figuring anything was better than this, Madison moved in to take her father's elbow and accept.

Dan simply nudged her away, instead yanking Paco by the elbow and whisking him to the center of the dance floor. Dragging his heels, Paco threw a helpless look at Madison, who covered her gaping mouth with one hand and threw him a confident thumbs-up with the other, approving with enthusiastic nodding.

CHAPTER 32

PACO

Amongst the couples crowding the dance floor, Paco felt oddly like a wallflower of a prom queen as Dan took the lead. His steps were remarkably good, though Paco had a hard time relaxing.

"Look," Dan said gruffly. "I'm sort of a cut-to-the-chase kind of guy."

"I respect that, sir," Paco said, nodding solemnly.

"I understand I owe you a debt."

At Dan's disarming words, Paco relaxed his tight shoulders, more confident in his steps. "No, not at all. You don't owe me anything. I was just . . ." Paco chose his words carefully, not sure how much Madison might have shared with her father. "I was just honoring a fellow service member. And a hell of a man."

Dan stared at him, narrowing his eyes as he digested the words. "Interesting," he said, letting the word hang for a second. "True enough, but not exactly the whole truth."

Feeling caught in the semblance of a lie, Paco fumbled to explain. "Sir, I'm—"

"No *sirs* between us." Dan glared back, insulted. "No *sir* or *mister*. You can forget all that shit right now. Call me Dan. Or—"

He paused for a moment to pull a small item from his breast pocket and place it in Paco's hand.

Taking a closer look, Paco stared at it in disbelief, trying to make sense of it through suddenly watery eyes. It was the photo. The only one of him, Jack, and Alex—intact and encased in a small silver frame.

Before he could ask, Dan continued. "Or you can also call me Dad."

Shocked, Paco had nothing to say.

Dan grunted. "Okay, maybe that's too much. How about you at least let me call you *son*?"

Closing the space between them, Dan swooped in for a hug, a heartfelt squeeze that stole Paco's breath. Overwhelmed with emotion, he hugged back very, very hard.

Before his tears could break free, Madison cut in.

"Hey," she said, wiping a rogue tear from Paco's eye. "I'm sorry to barge in on the moment, but the other members of our party have finally arrived."

After kissing Paco's cheek, she pointed to the double doors, where Alex was leading an elegantly gowned woman into the room.

"Yasmin!" Paco gasped as they approached. "What—"

Alex cut him off. "Don't worry. I've got twelve guards posted throughout. All entrances are covered, and nobody knows she's here. It's been a while since you two caught up," he said, handing her off to the man officially recognized as her husband.

In Yasmin's native tongue, she and Paco began to talk before he pulled her away to the dance floor. She struggled a little with the steps, but as he led her confidently, she relaxed with a smile.

Paco watched as Dan made his way to the bar, and admired Madison cuddled in Alex's arms. He mouthed a small *thank you* their way before the music swept them away as well.

CHAPTER 33

MADISON

Madison had enjoyed every minute of the wedding and the reception that followed. Seeing her dad dance with Paco. Meeting the woman who'd saved his life. Soaking in a moment to press against the solid muscles of one Mr. Alex Drake.

Gazing up at him, she was captivated. His handsome features and tender eyes looked back, and she could almost imagine they were alone.

"Isn't that Alex Drake?" she overheard someone say, which ticked up her anxiety to the point she hoped her hives didn't break out, seeing as she was in a sleeveless gown.

Alex pressed his warm cheek to hers. "Hey, how about we get some air?"

Relieved, Madison said, "I'd like that."

With his arm at the small of her back, he led her to an isolated balcony private enough for just the two of them. The brisk evening air chilled her into shivers, and she hugged herself, as the off-the-shoulder gown hardly held in the heat.

The satiny lining of Alex's jacket draped her with warmth as his kiss skimmed her neck. It was still warm with his heat.

"Better?" he asked.

"Mm-hmm," she said, smiling. Redolent of his cologne and his own scent, his jacket gave her all she needed to wrap it closer and soak him in.

"I've got something for you," Alex murmured in her ear, holding her tight from behind.

Madison looked back, noticing his gaze was fixed on the stone railing of the balcony. She turned to look and held her breath. On the railing was a small velvet jewelry box beckoning her with its distinctive blue hue.

Locked in place, Madison could only stare at the unmistakable Tiffany & Co. box. Her heart thundered, threatening to pound clear out of her chest.

This can't be happening.

As if reading her mind, Alex tightened his hold and nuzzled her ear. "It's not what you think," he said with a light peck. When she gave him a skeptical smile, he said, "Go ahead. Open it."

She took a few slow, unsteady steps toward it, as if she might scare it into flight if she moved too fast. Glancing back again, she was reassured by Alex motioning her forward with a nod.

Madison nodded too, if only to herself. Staring down at the velvety casing, she scooped the box into her hands. Prying the lid just a little, she built enough courage to open it.

Alex was indeed telling the truth. It wasn't at all what she thought. It was a hundred times more.

Where a ring could have been, a shiny new penny stood upright with a note tucked in the lid. When she propped the box all the way open, she could read each of the three little words.

I'm all in!

Madison's face blossomed with a huge smile as she took it all in.

After one night together with Alex, she'd made a wish, pouring her hope into the silent message—a shiny penny left behind. A crazy dream of forever being tied to a man who managed to steal her heart. And tonight, he'd wished it right back, promising his heart in return.

She turned back, finding Alex Drake coming as close as he ever had to a lie. There he was, before her on one knee. With a gasp, she covered her open mouth with a hand.

"Madison *Elizabeth* Taylor . . ."

It made her burst out in a sweet giggle, and not just from the amazing setting and proposal to come, but also because it was the first time she'd ever heard her entire name out loud when she wasn't in trouble. Yet somehow, she had the sneaking suspicion she was about to get in a whole lot of trouble. The man before her was the total package, offering her a life filled with risk and adventure, alive with perpetual seduction and unrivaled romance.

Sporting those charming dimples, he kept going. "I never imagined I could find love, or be loved, so fully and completely. From the day our worlds collided, I was forever changed, and I can't imagine a single day of the rest of my life without you." He held up a ring, whose brilliance and size seemed to pale in comparison only to the full moon above. "Please, Madison. Marry me."

Unable to speak or move, she simply nodded, letting the happiest tears stream down her cheeks.

Rising, Alex took her trembling hands with a sparkle in his eyes. "Is that a yes?"

Madison's smile widened, and she nodded as she whispered, "Yes, Alex. Yes."

After placing the ring on her finger, he wiped more tears with his thumbs as his hands cradled her face. His mouth descended on hers with a kiss, making her head swirl and her knees weak.

Is this real? To love and be so incredibly and unconditionally loved back?

But it was real. And she was his.

Several low voices pulled Alex from their kiss, and Madison from her thoughts. She pulled back slightly from his embrace, realizing they were no longer alone. Looking over, she giggled at the small audience of her family and very closest friends standing just inside the doorway.

Sheila leaned against Paco, confused and unsure. "Did my girl say yes?"

Alex nodded, squeezing Madison tighter to him.

At that nod, Paco pulled up his phone and gave Madison a loving look. "She said yes," he shouted into the phone.

A moment later, Madison jumped at the loud booms of fireworks overhead, popping in rapid succession as they lit up the night sky.

Sheila raced over to hug her bestie, handing over her bouquet and meeting Madison's regretful glance.

"I'm sorry," Madison said sincerely, not wanting to take anything away from Sheila's wedding day.

"Don't worry. Everyone thinks the fireworks are for me and Kent. Only we," she swirled her hand around at the gathering on the balcony, "know the truth."

Smiling, Madison accepted the arrangement, lavishly spilling over with roses and peonies.

"And speaking of truth, Little Miss *Curious*," Sheila said, prompting Madison's blush to burn its way up her cheeks. "The truth is, I couldn't be happier. And I get why you kept it on the down low, but I'll forgive it all if you promise me this—I get first crack at your wedding announcement."

"Deal!" Madison said with relief, beaming back at Alex, who tore his gaze away and began waving toward the door.

"Samantha!"

Sexy Samantha?

The woman approaching them was elegant and poised, and beaming with delight. Alex released Madison for a moment to accept Samantha's businesslike hug before handing her off to Madison, who was embraced with one much warmer.

"Well?" Samantha asked impatiently under her breath. Her gaze darted to Alex.

Without a word, Alex swept Madison's hand up in presentation, letting her admire it. "As always, your work is impeccable."

"Your work?" Madison asked.

"Madison, meet Samantha Hayes, the designer of your ring. She owns Hayes Fine Jewelers."

Hayes Fine Jewelers? The same jeweler who designs engagement rings for actresses and influencers? Heads of states and royals?

"You have no idea the lengths Alex went to keep this from the press," Samantha said with a laugh.

I've got some idea.

Alex reclaimed Madison, locking his strong arm around her waist. "I couldn't risk scaring you away. Nothing says *run for the hills* like a dozen reporters asking about an engagement."

They all laughed until Sheila chimed in. "To set the record straight, Madison has never run from this reporter."

Samantha handed a small box to the bride. "You must be Sheila. Congratulations. Sorry to crash your party and run, but when a client requests this, I make it a point to always deliver it personally. Now I'm off to London for the next ten days."

Delighted, Sheila popped the clasp on the hinged velvet box and pried it open. Inside was a golden gift certificate with her name filled in and signed by Alex, but no dollar amount.

"Thank you," she said repeatedly, though her confusion was still clear on her face.

Samantha leaned in, saying softly, "The technical term for that is a blank check."

After nearly taking out everyone's eardrums with her scream, Sheila grabbed Alex in a grateful chokehold he didn't seem to mind.

Eventually, she released him, putting a momentary halt to her gushing to hug Samantha. "You can't go!" Sheila said firmly. "You have to meet my husband. And have cake and champagne."

"Consider my arm twisted," Samantha said with a quick hug to both Alex and Madison.

Sheila followed suit, leaving a kiss on Madison's cheek and a smug comment whispered in her ear. "This certificate proves my point. Samantha *is* sexy."

Giggling, Madison glanced at her ring. "Yes, she is."

Sheila stepped away to lock arms with the sexy jeweler and lead her back inside.

As an endless stream of fireworks exploded in the sky and her heart pounded, Madison melted as Alex gave her another breathtaking kiss. He brushed a strand of hair behind her shoulder as he looked into her eyes.

"I love you, Madison."

Madison let her finger trace his jaw, finding a resting spot in the dimple of his chin. She was ready to expose one last tidbit she knew about Alex Drake—a namesake he shared with another man so very close to her heart. "I love you too, Alexander Jackson Drake."

With that, Madison and Alex shared another kiss—a bond that swept them through the night and into a new life, and adventure, together.

∼

Thank you for reading *Exposed*! I hope you love Alex and Madison as much as I do. (And, of course, Paco.) *Ready for the next adventure?* **Get BURNED Now!**

Keep going to read the first few chapters.

∼

If you loved Access and Exposed, you'll love Fallen Dom.

For Jake Russo, abandoning the past became his only future. It should have been his burden alone. But he had one cross to bear. Watching over Kathryn Chase . . . in secret.

Her unangelic guardian paying back a debt.

Available on All Platforms! **Get FALLEN DOM now!**

∼

Looking for another sexy billionaire? Meet Davis R. Black ... aka Richard. Some know him as a tech mogul. To Jaclyn, he's the King of the A-holes. Which is why this billionaire is hiding *his* in plain sight. Check out the first book in the Ruthless Billionaires Club.

Available on All Platforms! **Get RUTHLESS GAMES now!**

∼

Join Lexxi's VIP reader list to be the first to know of new releases, free books, special prices, and other giveaways!

Free hot romances & happily ever afters delivered to your inbox.
https://www.lexxijames.com/freebies

BURNED

AN ALEX DRAKE NOVEL

CHAPTER 1

MADISON

Manhattan

Crouched awkwardly in the small space between the watercooler and the wall, Madison couldn't help looking up at the half-filled tank in disbelief.

They're actually gossiping next to the watercooler? How horribly on the nose.

Deflated, she flinched at the sting of each rumor she overheard from her unintended surveillance spot. And the question she mentally kicked herself over wasn't how could this have happened, but how could it not?

Somehow, she'd managed to convince herself that the news of her upcoming nuptials would be barely newsworthy in the engagements section of the *New York Times*.

Ha!

She'd even helped craft the matter-of-fact snippet, certain it would be buried beneath the actual full-blown wedding announcements, not to mention the reports of stock surges and gripping national news.

Her best friend, Sheila—the up-and-coming reporter

Madison had promised the story to—had made every change Madison requested. In the end, the announcement was limited to a single line.

BILLIONAIRE CEO ALEX DRAKE AND DGI ANALYST MADISON TAYLOR TO WED

Sheila had been promised the scoop, and Madison Taylor was a woman of her word. She held tight to her integrity, no matter how uncomfortable it was. And it was definitely uncomfortable . . . hiding in a corner behind the coffee bar in the break room of Drake Global Industries.

Madison sucked in a silent breath, taking in this long, exhausting day had begun well before the crack of dawn. Glancing at row of international clocks on the wall, the one set for New York time hadn't yet hit eleven a.m.

Awesome.

Texts had begun blowing up her cell phone about five a.m., a total of several hundred because apparently her number was splayed across the Times Square Jumbotron. .

How do I get my number unlisted from the world? Just a small-town girl engaged to a billionaire. Nothing to see here, folks. Nothing to see.

Madison wiggled her toes, afraid they were falling asleep. *I should've called in sick.*

Sick. Or freaked out. *Tomayto, tomahto.*

None of this was as bad as she'd imagined. No, it was so horribly, awfully, painfully much worse.

How this should have gone down was with her busting out a magnanimous can of whoop-ass on her slanderous coworkers the moment she heard the first barb. But this was Alex's company, not hers. And temper tantrums at the office from his new fiancée wouldn't be a good look for either of them. Confronting her detractors would create a situation the press would undoubtedly blow completely out of proportion.

Instead, the women's incoming voices with her name on their lips as they approached the break room had rushed her ass to retreat to a corner that, between you and me, it barely managed to squeeze into.

And there she remained, wedged between the wall and the watercooler. In competitive hide and seek, this space would have rated a C+ at best. But if she were very quiet and still, her secret hideaway would work.

"Madison Taylor," one of them said with disdain. "Who would have thought it? All sweet and innocent, and fucking the boss the whole time."

Madison peeked out as best she could, eyeing the trio of women she'd never even met. After all, over a thousand DGI employees worked at the headquarters here in Manhattan.

Who cares what they say?

Annoyed at herself, she stifled a snort. That was a stupid question. She cared. Way more than every brain cell in her ducked-down head said she should.

I don't even know these women.

But if middle school had taught her anything—other than how to use a tampon, that hair gel and eyebrow tweezing should be done sparingly, and that the little boy you crushed on so hard and wished you could marry someday was batting for the other team—it was that where a trail of mean girls started, endless swarms of them followed.

"I'll bet Little Miss Prim and Proper does it every which way. Like a pet on some diamond-studded leash. You know, a girlfriend of mine dated him."

Unimpressed, Mean Girl Number Two responded with another slap in the face. "Who hasn't?"

The third chimed in. "Yeah, he's had more women spread eagle than the American Society of Obstetrics. And does that man have a dark side. Kink to the core. Only one way she's marriage material."

Madison's frustration and anger slid to the back seat as her curiosity called shotgun, with a flutter of hope that the next words spoken would be *true love*.

The third girl snickered. "Ménage."

"Not *à trois*, if that's where you're going."

Madison let out a silent exhale of relief.

"More like *à cinq*."

Her eyes popped open wide. *Five? Really? Oh, come on. Do I walk like I've been done every which way to Sunday?*

"Now we know why there are so many chairs in the boardroom," one of them said, which drew a titter of cruel laughter from the others.

Madison rolled her eyes. This was too much. With the air ripe with premium roast and vicious gossip, she was losing her cool. It didn't help that these women were taking the longest coffee break ever, lazily drawing out their time—and Madison's as well.

All I wanted was some freaking water.

Her options were dwindling, but she could always confront them. Jump out and defend her honor, slaying them with an accusatory "gotcha" finger pointing straight at their shocked faces as she exclaimed, "Aha! I heard every word."

So what if it lost its impact because she'd been listening way too long?

Jump up and confront them? At this point, standing might be its own challenge. Hiding had been a bad idea from the start, one that grew worse with each minute she stayed put.

No amount of yoga or deep breathing would prevent her cramped legs from falling asleep. And, of course, the women were taking their sweet damn time finishing up, because God forbid they actually get back to work.

Madison said one silent prayer after another that the women would leave before her legs completely gave out. Impatiently, she squatted, waiting out the swarms of prickles running up and down her calves and thighs, willing herself not to fall flat on her ass when her muscles finally gave out.

After about a million years, the gossips collected their coffee cups overflowing with freshly slung mud before inching their way into the hall, continuing their obnoxiously loud chatter and giving Madison a reprieve.

A much-needed reprieve that would have to wait even longer. It would seem that with all her patience and silent fuming, her wedged-in body was now hopelessly stuck.

Huffing, or semi-hyperventilating, she sucked in a long breath and gripped the watercooler with one hand while resting her other palm on the wall.

Madison's first heave to push herself up seemed promising. At halfway through heave number two, she stopped short to avoid the sloshing tank from tipping completely over. And when another set of footsteps casually strolled into the break room, she did what any self-respecting junior analyst marrying the boss would do in her place. She froze.

"Hello?" the sultry voice called out, undoubtedly noticing the still sloshing tank gurgling, complete with big, blaring bubbles and all.

Shyly, Madison peered around the tank as subtly as she could, watching the slow sashay of a five-foot-ten-inch supermodel with ass-length hair heading straight toward her.

Crap.

The woman who certainly didn't need the five-inch stilettos rocked them like the world was her runway. She moved like magical fairy dust had touched one of *Charlie's Angels*, endowing her with a crazy blend of beauty, boobs, and even maybe the softest touch of badass that Madison admired.

This woman set Madison's nerves on edge as she stooped before her, eyeing her up and down with a grin. "Everything okay?"

"Oh. Yes." Madison nodded, struggling to appear casual and nonchalant. "I just, um, dropped something."

The ruby-red lips of the strange woman widened with intrigue as she barely glanced around the floor. "And then sat on it? Is it an egg? If you're a golden goose, I'm claiming you."

The stranger stood and extended her hand. Madison graciously accepted the hoist of her remarkably strong and effortless pull.

The relief of standing pushed an uncontrollable sigh from Madison's throat. "*Ah*, thank you." She rubbed at the pins and needles in her thighs, pointedly glancing down. "See? No golden egg."

Her rescuer smirked. "Well, I guess I won't be your captor, then."

"Good thing too, as I'm already spoken for."

"So I hear," the woman teased, arching a perfectly shaped brow.

When Madison's face fell and she ducked her head, the stranger tipped her head back up with a couple of soft fingers beneath her chin.

"Yeah, the trio in the hall weren't exactly curbing their enthusiasm." Confidently, she stroked Madison's arm. "Don't let them get to you. Jealousy is *très déclassé*."

Soothed, Madison wasn't sure what to say in response. "Thanks. I appreciate that. Can I treat you to a coffee?" she asked, offering up the selection of coffees displayed next to a dozen Keurig machines.

"Actually, I don't do coffee. I just came to recycle my water bottle." Giving the clear plastic enough of a squeeze to make it crackle, the woman placed the empty Evian in the recycling bin. "And I should really get back."

"Well, thanks again for helping me up." Extending a hand, she introduced herself. "I'm Madison."

The woman clasped it in both of hers, smoothing a thumb

against her skin. "I know," she said, leaning close and flashing a knowing grin. "Pretty sure everyone knows."

A short silence hung between them while their eye contact teetered to awkward.

Finally, the woman released Madison's hand, offering her own cryptic introduction. "Just call me *J*."

"Jay?"

"Mm-hmm. You know . . . like J-Lo."

Madison smiled, finding the name fitting, considering the woman carried herself with the confidence and poise of a known triple threat. "Well, *J*, it was nice to meet you."

"You too."

J began a very catwalk departure, pausing only for a moment as Madison called out, "See you around."

With a slow turn and a suggestive grin, *J* gave her a solemn but friendly reassurance. "Definitely."

She then disappeared down the hall, leaving Madison with an unsettled knot in her chest.

Without a doubt, the underbelly of the DGI grapevine would be buzzing with everyone's take on *Junior Analyst Beds the Boss*. Yup, this was the perfect way to grow a budding career built with hard work and integrity, taken seriously at every step for the smart, savvy, growing businesswoman she was.

Riiight, her inner voice said before another thought hit her. *I could leave.*

Leave? For how long . . . a day? A week? It didn't matter. Everyone knew. *Everyone*. And the few people who didn't—like the preppers avoiding the news or the castaways on deserted islands—offered little solace that this would all blow over.

Desperate to shake off her plummet into the freefall of anxiety, Madison weighed her options. Fresh air was always a good call.

Tempted by the bright outdoors peeking through from the lobby exit door, Madison took a determined detour to a street vendor on the corner. Hurried and trying not to make eye contact with anyone, she bought a pre-wrapped salad and a glass bottle of Coke—the kind with real sugar—because it was that kind of a day.

Armed with lunch, Madison slunk back to her office for a little alone time to focus on two side-by-side oversize computer monitors filled with lots and lots and lots of data.

Because data didn't gossip, and data didn't judge. And the mountain of glorious data at her disposal was enough to hide behind for the rest of the day. Alone. Diligently working and not obsessing over the ticking time bomb of an expiration date for this very precious and amazing job.

CHAPTER 2

ALEX

"Five hundred million?" Alex Drake asked, staring at his computer monitor while barely paying attention to the conversation from the speakerphone.

Preoccupied, he wasn't exactly on top of the discussion, but like the CEO he was, responded decisively. "Sounds fine," he muttered, approving who the hell knew what. For all he knew, he'd agreed to bribes, sex toys, and a year's worth of hookers for the Senate.

The email that had snagged his attention sat unopened for several moments, his finger hovering with uncertainty, because approving whatever half a billion dollars was buying was an easier decision than opening that email.

Labeled PRIVATE, it had been sent by a ghost he hadn't heard from in ten years, the only person he'd thought about all that time with the same interest as he'd wondered about his close friend's little sister. Madison had become his fixation. But *J. Stone* had been an unclosed chapter of his past.

With the shame of idiocy settling in and the insistence that there was no fear in reading an email, he finally clicked it open.

Within the email was a video clip taken from the DGI headquarters lobby not ten minutes ago. The *J* from the email was front and center, strolling through the lobby of the headquarters of his multibillion-dollar empire as if she owned the place.

Is there some corner of her misguided mind that thinks she owns me as well?

With thoughtful intensity, Alex studied the footage frame by frame, desperate to analyze the three-minute clip. The statuesque woman made long, stately strides to the security desk. Fife, DGI's chief of security, stood to greet her and pointed to the lobby restroom. She thanked him and stepped away.

In her natural sashay, she made her way to the ladies' room, waving her arm back to the camera and holding up three fingers. She disappeared behind the door.

A sound of gruff irritation left his lips, followed by, "Shit," as he jumped to his feet. The video was done.

"No to the orphanage donation?" his vice president of corporate charities asked, shy surprise in her tone.

"What?" Briefly, Alex focused, mentally flipping through the slides he'd scanned a few hours earlier. Recalling the line in question, he rushed to agree.

"No, no. We're good. Approved for the orphanage, and I've gone through your analysis. Well done. Approved for all charity requests for the next six months, but let's keep a close eye on the burn rate for the food banks. I'd like to revisit in thirty days in case we need to send them more."

Rising to his feet with a finger ready, he said, "I need to cut this short." He blurted out a *thank you* before killing the call and taking his private elevator downstairs to the lobby.

With a quick glance around as he tried to appear nonchalant, Alex swiftly stepped into the ladies' room.

An observant glance at the orthopedic shoes revealed beneath the door of stall one urged him to rush past the closed door, eager to avoid any face-to-face meetings. He ignored the usual sounds commonplace in bathrooms.

At stall three, the closed door he was sure was vacant gave with the slightest push of his fingers. Having said a silent *thank God*, he entered.

Empty.

He took a doubtful look into the pristinely clean bowl, certain no further exploration was necessary, but made a mental note to give bonuses to the cleaning staff.

When the toilet from two stalls over flushed, Alex shut the door. Behind it, he found a note, recognizing the ornate penmanship.

Alex

Tamping down the faintest trace of a sentimental thought or emotion, he snatched down the taped note and flipped it open. One word was carefully scrawled, with a heart over the *i*.

Congratulations

Alex flipped it over, diligent in making sure he hadn't missed more.

J wasn't his past. She was ancient fucking history, returning to taunt him in his own lobby while leaving behind no trace except an email and a cryptic note about his impending nuptials. It didn't make sense.

Dumbfounded, Alex couldn't make heads or tails of it, but was certain this wouldn't be her last word. Slipping the note in his pocket, he stepped out of the stall without checking to be sure he was now alone.

"Oh!" the elegant older woman said in shock. She wore a smart blue suit that matched her wide eyes, and the orthopedic shoes he'd glimpsed beneath the stall door.

Grateful that he didn't recognize her, Alex gave her a shy smile. Clinging to a hope, a prayer, and blind faith that her thick glasses made him indistinguishable in a lineup, he apologized and excused himself, briskly moving past her.

"Ahem." Her expression stern, she cleared her throat and glanced pointedly at his hands, then at the sink.

He took a begrudging step to the sink, not bothering to explain he hadn't actually used the toilet in the women's restroom. He wrapped up as soon as he'd mentally finished his ABCs and headed back to his office, pretending, as Fife did, that he hadn't been spotted.

Between the mysterious note and the uneasy feeling that, as CEO of the company, he might be adding another idiosyncrasy to the growing list of rumored ones he knew of, he welcomed an incoming call from Mark Donovan.

The man might be his evil arch nemesis in public as CEO of Excelsior/Centurion, but to Alex, he was one of only a handful of very close friends.

"Hey, Mark. I see you're calling from your cell, so may I assume bail money isn't required?"

"Not this time." Mark's tone was far from easygoing as he blew out a heavy breath. "Listen, we need to talk. It's a guy thing."

It's a guy thing wasn't a guy thing. It was code. Mark needed Alex's ear, and it had to be somewhere secure and away from both of their offices. In these situations, they met at an off-the-grid secure facility both of them knew the route to by heart.

Frowning, Alex kept his voice even and light as he said, "Sure."

Tonight, they were supposed to be heading out for a weekend getaway. Alex and Madison would be meeting Mark and his wife, Jess, at their luxury cabin hidden deep in the Adirondacks. This would change the plans.

"How about you ask Jess to grab Madison?" Alex said. "I know she would love a girls' drive up." Caution prevented him from saying anything else.

"Perfect," Mark said quickly. "You let Madison know, and I'll tell Jess."

"When do you want to get together?"

"You know. See ya."

From the *see ya*, Alex did know. Those two words translated to a time. *Five thirty*.

∼

Ready for more? **Get BURNED Now!**

ABOUT THE AUTHOR

Lexxi James is a best-selling author of romantic suspense. Her feats in multi-tasking include binge watching Netflix and sucking down a cappuccino in between feverish typing and loads of laundry.

She lives in Ohio with her teen daughter and the sweetest man in the universe. She loves to hear from readers!

www.LexxiJames.com

facebook.com/LexxiJames
twitter.com/LexxiJamesBooks
instagram.com/lexxijamesbooks
amazon.com/Lexxi-James/e/B07VQWWX19
pinterest.com/LexxiJames

Printed in Great Britain
by Amazon